Mary Angela Dickens

Cross Currents

Vol. III

Mary Angela Dickens

Cross Currents
Vol. III

ISBN/EAN: 9783337066994

Printed in Europe, USA, Canada, Australia, Japan

Cover: Foto ©Andreas Hilbeck / pixelio.de

More available books at **www.hansebooks.com**

CROSS CURRENTS.

A Novel.

BY

MARY ANGELA DICKENS.

IN THREE VOLUMES.

VOL. III.

LONDON: CHAPMAN AND HALL,
LIMITED.
1891.

CHARLES DICKENS AND EVANS,
CRYSTAL PALACE PRESS.

CROSS CURRENTS.

CHAPTER I.

Two days after the Sunday on which Helen, Humphrey, and Selma dined at the Cornishes', Mervyn Ferris was left alone at home with the prospect of a solitary fortnight, and Mrs. Cornish asked her to come and spend the time with them. Roger, whose business arrangements at that time were rather unsettled, was a good deal at home just then, and the ice having been so thoroughly broken between them, Selma's old lover and her enthusiastic little adorer found a constant bond of sympathy, and an unfailing topic for tête-à-tête conversations, in Selma's perfections.

The bitter and unpardoning animosity which

had lurked in the tone of almost every one who had hitherto spoken or written to him of Selma —though any open expression of such a feeling to him had from the very first received a simple and decided check—had been a constant distress and reproach to Roger. That she should lose affection and respect for what he looked upon as entirely his own fault, hurt him almost as though he himself had actually done something to lower her in popular estimation. The bitter pain of his first disappointment was past for him now, although he hardly realised the fact ; the element of reverent uncertainty which had been so prominent a characteristic of his love, had come to his help in his trouble, and he had grown, with time, to look upon the girl he had lost as an altogether superior order of being—to be admired and worshipped as such, but to be thought of no longer with the simple, protecting love which such a man as Roger Cornish gives to his wife.

To hear her talked of as Mervyn talked of

her, to be able to dwell on her beauty and her general perfection was, to him, like the restoration of his own self-respect. That the conversation which began with Selma should not invariably end with her, was not so wonderful as it seemed, on reflection, to Roger.

Mervyn's visit to the Cornishes was drawing to a close, when Helen, coming in one afternoon about tea-time, as she often did, found the whole party assembled in the drawing-room. Roger and Mervyn were both there, and, after a few minutes, a most unusual fit of silence and abstraction seemed to come over Helen, which lasted until she found herself in Sylvia's bedroom, whither the latter had conducted her to inspect something or other — Helen was not quite sure what. She was standing with the recent purchase in question—a hat—in her hand, looking at it vaguely, when she said, slowly :

" Sylvia, have you noticed anything ? "

Sylvia looked at her quickly.

" What sort of thing, Helen ? " she asked,

looking down again at the hat, on which Helen's eyes were also fixed.

"Roger and—and Mervyn," said Helen. And then she and Sylvia looked up simultaneously, their eyes met, and the new hat was nearly demolished as they suddenly and vigorously embraced. "Oh, my dear!" cried Helen, joyfully. "Is it really, do you think? How long has it been going on? Oh, tell me all about it, do!"

"We all think so," returned Sylvia, eagerly, as though she were only too delighted to talk about it. "I don't believe they've any idea of it themselves, yet; it would take them ever so long to think of such a thing, you know. But wouldn't it be delightful?"

"Nothing could possibly be better," answered Helen. "Selma will never really forgive herself until he is married; and perhaps when there's no doubt as to his being quite cured. you'll all forgive her, Sylvia?" she finished, wistfully.

"We have—we have quite forgiven her," protested Sylvia; "if it is because she can't forgive herself that she hasn't been here since that Sunday, I think she ought to make an effort, Nell. Mother has spoken about it several times."

"She is so busy," said Helen, apologetically, not mentioning that she had several times made energetic, but entirely unsuccessful, attempts to get her sister to go with her to make the call on her aunt which mere civility required. "She is so very busy, Sylvia.

There was a moment's silence, and then Helen, returning to the topic from which they had gone off at a tangent, said :

"Oh, I shall be so anxious to hear how they get on, Sylvia—Mervyn and Roger, I mean. I suppose I had better not say anything to Selma yet, in case it should be a false hope."

"I wouldn't, certainly," returned Sylvia, promptly, thinking that Selma might very well wait. "I'm so glad you noticed it, Helen. I've been longing to talk to you about it. We are so pleased."

But the Cornishes' satisfaction was nothing to Helen's. It seemed to her that Roger's marriage was just the one thing that could and would put everything straight again, and lift the shadow of self-reproach from Selma's mind. That Selma suffered greatly from an exaggerated feeling of remorse and shame at her own conduct towards Roger, was the dominant principle in Helen's consideration of her sister at present, and had coloured all her impressions for many months. She would have hailed the news of his marriage to any one, almost, with joy, and she could hardly restrain herself from telling Selma of the probabilities that very evening. She contented herself, however, with mentioning that Mervyn was still with the Cornishes, and that Roger had still very little occupation, placing the two facts significantly near to one another ; and during the weeks that followed, as her hopes rose higher, and her satisfaction increased every day, she never came from the Cornishes' without having something to tell Selma in which the names Mervyn and Roger occurred in close proximity.

Helen was anxious that her sister should call with her, because of what Sylvia had said, and because Mrs. Cornish had several times hinted as to her non-appearance, and also because she wished her to have a chance of seeing with her own eyes what was likely to happen—as she might easily do any day at the Cornishes' house, where Mervyn was constantly to be found. But Selma was never able to go; all Helen's representations and arrangements for her were quietly put aside with a reference to her work.

Nobody who knew how her days were spent could have said that her words were an idle excuse. Tyrrell had arranged for the series of matinées for which she had begged—as an experiment, he announced—and though he altogether declined to hear even of more than one every fortnight, the amount of work which Selma contrived to get out of them was positively amazing to him. She rehearsed with him, and she rehearsed with the company as often as she could persuade him to call a rehearsal; and he knew that she must study hard at home to arrive in so short a time at the results she attained. She went into every minutest detail of dress, which could possibly affect the correctness of the picture she was to make, with a feverish thoroughness.

Miss Tyrrell's lamentations over her were bitter and incessant. After her success as Bianca, invitations for all such "quiet" entertainments as were given in Lent showered upon her through that lady, and she refused them one and all. She was too busy, she said, to go out in the afternoon, and too tired after her day's work to go out in the evening.

"She has a chance for which any other girl would give ten years of her life," bewailed Miss Tyrrell as she received one refusal after another. "And she is simply throwing herself away over this ridiculous mania for improvement. Of course,

I know," she added, as Tyrrell's mouth took a cynical twist at this very plain speaking, " of course, I know that an artist must be devoted to her art; but still, I do not see why Selma should refuse the Duchess's dinner "— which was the immediate cause of Miss Tyrrell's outbreak. "She is absolutely overworking herself, too, John. I thought her looking quite haggard the other day, and altogether strained and tired. She'll lose her beauty if she isn't careful, and then what will all this work do for her ? "

John Tyrrell, to whom this harangue was addressed one morning at breakfast, made no attempt to reply to it. Selma was, in fact, something of a perplexity to him. He was well-used to what his sister defined as her "mania for improvement," but there was something about her manner of working lately which was new to him — something which he had once found himself defining as " desperate." The word, though he dismissed it the first time it occurred to him with a little contemptuous smile, came back to him again and again; and the more keenly and carefully he watched her, the less he understood her. It annoyed him, and it also annoyed him that, often as they met for purposes of rehearsal, Selma's whole mind was invariably concentrated on the matter in hand, and she neither heard nor understood him when he attempted to "waste the time," as she expressed it, in desultory personal conversation.

It was a bright, warm, April day, nearly two months after the family dinner party at Mrs. Cornish's, and into Selma's pretty sitting-room the soft spring air floated through the open window with a pleasant suggestion of country fields and flowers in its breath. But its gentle touch was unnoticed by Selma; she was walking up and down the room, her face flushed and tired-looking, and with a look in her eyes as though the concentration she was giving to the new part she was studying so indefatigably were a painful effort of will. She had been working for nearly two hours, and the flush on her cheeks was fading and leaving it very white, when there was a knock at the door, and the servant told her that Mr. Tyrrell was downstairs, and had asked to see her.

"The dining-room door was open, miss, and Mr. Tyrrell said he would go in there as he wanted to see you on business," added the girl, apologetically.

"Very well, thank you, Mary," said Selma, as she went quickly downstairs, wondering a little what the business could be that was so important. It was the first time Tyrrell had been to the house to see her.

"I hope there's nothing wrong, Mr. Tyrrell?" she began, nervously, as she entered the room.

Tyrrell was standing with his back to the door looking at a picture—a sketch of Selma which Humphrey had done long ago, and given to Helen. He turned quickly as she spoke, and came towards her.

"How do you do?" he said, quietly, as they shook hands. "Don't look so anxious, there is nothing wrong."

"I am getting nervous, I believe," she said, as she sat down, with a little laugh, which was somehow not quite natural. "I was afraid something might have happened——"

"To give you more work?" he interrupted, looking at her curiously.

"No, no, indeed," she protested, feverishly. "On the contrary, I was afraid something might have happened to postpone the next matinée."

He sat down close to her, and said, with what seemed to Selma kindly solicitude:

"Selma, you are looking very tired. Am I overworking my 'leading lady'?"

"No!" she cried, vehemently, turning her face away from him, and pressing her hands against her pale cheeks as the colour flew to them. "I'm not tired — not in the least! And if I were, you know that it's only a necessary part of it. You said it was a struggle, and a constant effort! You said so!"

She faced him again as if defying him to notice the inconsistency of her words, and he understood at once that she was referring to the words he had once said to her about an artist's life—the life from which she had then been turning away.

"Did I!" he said, quietly. "I said then, at the same time perhaps, that the struggle brought its own reward! Do you find it so?"

She was still looking straight at him, but apparently she did not see him; at least, she was quite unconscious of his eyes. Her colour came and went, her lips set themselves, her eyes were dark and burning. At last, as though she forced it from herself, her answer came, vehement, almost passionate in its protestation.

"Yes!" she cried. "Yes, yes, yes!" Then apparently becoming conscious of herself and her excitement, she rose abruptly, and going to the window, stood there, with her back towards him, looking out.

He did not speak to her. He was quite aware that he had had a glimpse at the real Selma, as she was at present, such as he had not had for months, and he was more annoyed than ever with himself for not being able to understand what he had seen. He was still reflecting, when she turned again with all the excitement gone from her face.

"I beg your pardon," she said, with a faint smile. "I'm afraid I've been gushing. There is something you want to talk about, isn't there?"

There was a good deal about which Tyrrell wanted to talk — about which he had wanted to talk for some time; but, above all things, he despised a man who risked a hair's-breadth for want of patience, and he said:

"Yes. I came to tell you that Arnold will design your dresses for Pauline if you have settled nothing about them yet. He must have an answer to-night "—Tyrrell did not mention that the obligation was of his own making—" so I thought I had better see you this afternoon."

"How kind of you!" said Selma, gratefully. "Don't think me very ungrateful if I say that my brother-in-law is doing them for me, and I won't trouble Mr. Arnold. He is very kind, but it seems to me that he hasn't much idea of character. I'm afraid, though," she added, hesitatingly, and with that deference in her tone with which she always considered a proposition of his, " I'm afraid you would have liked him to do them as you've taken all this trouble about it?"

" I don't care in the least," he replied, with a slight smile. " Your brother-in-law's designs are always excellent."

" Come up and see them, and have some

tea," she said. "Humphrey is taking a little holiday, and he will be delighted to see you, and so will Helen. They are both in the studio."

She had risen as she spoke; but he did not follow her example immediately. He sat looking up at her as she stood in the fading sunlight of the April afternoon.

"I came to see you," he said.

"But you are not in a hurry? Oh, do come!"

"I want to talk to you, Selma."

Her face changed instantly.

"Oh, I beg your pardon!" she said. "I did not know there was anything else. What is it?"

He looked at her for another instant, and then he rose abruptly.

"I dare say it will keep," he said. "I shall be delighted to go upstairs. Oh, by the way," he went on, "my sister sent you this, and said you were to send an answer. She also said that she would not write to you, as she left it to your common-sense to decide. I suppose, however, that your common-sense and hers are likely to decide differently."

His smile as he spoke was not a pleasant one. He knew better than to hurry Selma into a social position which she did not care to fill; but her steady refusal of the invitations she received annoyed him little less than it annoyed his sister.

"I — am I to send an answer by you?" asked Selma, looking up from the imposing card of invitation she had drawn from its envelope. "It's a fancy dress ball!"

"One of the biggest things of the season," he assented. "No, you'd better think about it and write."

And then, as she turned with a smile and a little shake of the head, he opened the door for her, and followed her upstairs.

"We hear that Humphrey's Academy picture is capitally hung," said Selma, as they went. "I hope——" she opened the studio door as she spoke, and stopped suddenly.

The next moment Mervyn Ferris, who was calling on Helen, had placed her cup of tea hastily upon the table, and had rushed across the room in her most impulsive way, and was embracing Selma, unobtrusively, but with something almost tremulous in her vehemence, while Helen and Humphrey shook hands with Tyrrell.

"You dearest dear," she said, not the less enthusiastically because the presence of Tyrrell, who was almost a stranger to her, caused her to utter the words in a vehement whisper. Then, releasing Selma, she said, shyly: "How do you do, Mr. Tyrrell?" And as he, having shaken hands with her with the faintest possible smile of amusement, followed Helen to the tea-table, she turned to Selma once more, and gave her another furtive little hug. "I thought I was never going to see you again," she went on. "Are you always going to be so busy? I've been here ever so many times, and they've always told me that you were at work, or at rehearsal, or busy about a dress or something. Do you know I haven't seen you since — since" — Mervyn faltered, stopped, and crimsoned. She and Selma had not met since the Sunday dinner at Mrs. Cornish's.

But Selma did not colour. Perhaps it was the pale gravity of her face and the curious quiet of her manner that gave Mervyn's eyes, as she looked at her, a slightly deprecating and wistful expression.

"I am very busy," answered Selma, simply. "Have you been here long, Mervyn?"

Mervyn made no reply. Her expressive little face was raised to speak when all at once it changed suddenly and completely. She was facing the door to which Selma's back was turned, and she had seen Roger Cornish come into the room.

"I thought I might come up," he said,

apologetically, as he shook hands with Helen, who, having given Tyrrell the cup of tea she had been pouring for him, had come forward with a smile to meet her brother-in-law. "I didn't know——"

He broke off, not liking to say that he had not expected to find any one beside themselves. He shook hands with Selma, and then he turned to Mervyn, and there was something in his look and manner as he did so, something in the eyes she lifted for a moment to his face, which made Helen glance triumphantly at her sister as she stood next to Mervyn, with a delighted conviction that the moment for which she had waited so impatiently had come at last. It was quite a disappointment to her to see that Selma had turned and moved suddenly away to where Humphrey and Tyrrell were standing talking together — a strikingly contrasted pair.

"I don't believe she saw," thought Helen.

There was a curious mutual interest and

liking between Humphrey Cornish and John Tyrrell, utterly at variance as were their schemes and ideals of life. Each man was conscious that there was more in the other than was easily to be fathomed ; Humphrey believed that the best of John Tyrrell had never been drawn out, and Tyrrell liked and respected the quiet painter without troubling himself to define the reason. They met seldom enough, but when they did meet, they had always plenty to say to one another ; and as Selma joined them now, Humphrey, who was speaking, did not break off, though his smile included her instantly in the conversation. It was Selma who interrupted him, abruptly :

"Humphrey," she said, " Mr. Tyrrell would like to see the Pauline sketches."

At the first sound of her voice, high-pitched, and almost harsh, though not loud, both men turned simultaneously to look at her. Then Humphrey glanced quickly from her face to where Roger and Mervyn still stood together, dilating to one another on the extraordinarily accidental character of their meeting, and saying, quietly :

" With pleasure, Selma. They are on this table," led the way to the other end of the room.

" What a capital studio you have here !" observed Tyrrell, as he followed him with Selma.

John Tyrrell had come to the house that afternoon determined, if possible, to get some clue to the indescribable change which he had noticed in Selma. He had only seen Roger Cornish once — on the October afternoon when he had gone to Selma with her release from her first professional engagement, and she had proudly introduced him to the man she was to marry — but he had known "the colonial fellow" again the instant he had appeared in the doorway, though until that moment he had had no idea that he was in London. The sight of her old lover, and the strange ring in her voice as she spoke to

Humphrey, taken in combination, had not only given him—as it seemed to him—the clue he wanted, but had let in a flood of light upon the position, of which he himself, John Tyrrell, was, in his own calculations, the centre figure. It was a light which not only roused all his intellectual faculties, but which stimulated, as they were not often stimulated now, all the calculating impulses into which he had subdued his passions; but as he uttered his complimentary comment on the studio, and strolled with Selma across the room, it would have been impossible to tell that anything in the least unusual was passing in his mind.

Humphrey silently produced the sketches, and Selma talked about them, describing the material and the colouring she proposed to use, rapidly, and rather incoherently, answered now and then by an appreciative word or two from Tyrrell. Humphrey had not spoken, and had hardly looked up from the sketches, when Helen, from the other end of the room, said:

"Humphrey, will you come here for a moment and tell Roger something?"

As he left them, with a word of excuse, silence fell upon Selma and Tyrrell. Selma, standing in shadow, was looking at the little group near the tea-table where Humphrey had joined, not Roger, but Helen. Tyrrell looked at her for a moment, and then followed the direction of her eyes. He saw Roger with Mervyn's teacup in his hand, his face towards them; he saw him bend down and give it her, and then, sitting down in the chair next her, lean forward and speak to her — the words themselves were lost in the words which were passing between Helen and Humphrey; but Roger's face, as he spoke, was plainly visible. Then Tyrrell turned and looked at Selma; and, as he saw the expression on her face, his own grew resolute and determined. His mouth set itself for a moment like iron, and there was a most unusual flash in his eyes.

"The sketches are excellent," he said,

lightly, turning away from her, and taking one in his hand again. "If you could make up your mind to that ball, now, either of these would be perfect."

She started at the sound of his voice, and looked round hurriedly as if to see if he had been looking at her. Then, as though she had hardly heard what he said, she answered vaguely, and as if only anxious to make conversation of any kind :

"The ball? Oh yes, the fancy ball. Tell me all about it, Mr. Tyrrell. I've never seen one."

"Then it would amuse you," he said, carelessly. "It is a pretty sight, and this will be magnificent. Lady Winslow always does things well."

"She is very handsome, isn't she?" said Selma, in a tone of the deepest interest, as she moved her chair a little so that she no longer saw the group by the tea-table.

"Well, no," returned Tyrrell, deliberately.

"You must be thinking of some one else. Lady Winslow is the ugliest woman in London."

The conversation which followed would have filled Miss Tyrrell with a hope that light was dawning on Selma at last. She kept up the conversation then started on Countesses and balls with a feverish eagerness and excitement, putting all kinds of questions on each subjects to Tyrrell whenever the talk seemed in danger of flagging. She was so deeply absorbed that Helen called her twice unheeded, and then came and put her hand on her shoulder.

"I'm so sorry to interrupt you, dear," she said. "I know how anxious you are about the Pauline dresses, but Mervyn is going."

Roger was going, too, it appeared, and Mervyn's eyes, as she said good-bye to Selma, were even more deprecating than when she kissed her first.

A few minutes after Tyrrell also said good-bye.

"By-the-bye," he said to Selma, as he took

leave, "Sybilla tells me that you don't mean to come to us on the second?"

Selma shook her head with a faint smile. The occasion in question was Miss Tyrrell's first large "at home" of the season.

"I shall have Pauline so much on my mind," she said.

"I am sorry!" he answered, gravely, and then he shook hands with Helen and Humphrey, and went away, and, as soon as he was gone, Selma, saying that she had a great deal to do before dinner, ran quickly upstairs.

As the door closed behind her, and Helen and Humphrey were left alone together, the former turned a radiant face towards her husband.

"I wonder whether she noticed," she cried. "I thought she looked rather odd and excited when she kissed Mervyn. Well, at any rate," with a happy little laugh, "I should think she would soon know now. Wasn't it delightful that they should meet here like that? Oh, poor dear, how pleased she will be!"

Humphrey was putting his sketches together with a rather grave and preoccupied air.

"I wonder!" he said, apparently in answer to his wife's first words. "I wonder!"

During the next two or three days that same grave, preoccupied air returned to Humphrey again and again, and Helen thought he must be meditating a new picture. To facilitate his meditations she left him as much as possible alone, expecting each evening that, as she sat with him while he smoked, he would deliver himself, according to his custom, first of a few slow words—few and far between—which should gradually grow under her very womanly and loving, if somewhat uncomprehending, sympathy to a full description of the picture which was growing in his mind; a description which he usually seemed to put into words as much for his own sake as for hers. But no such words came from him during these days, though, when Helen left him alone, he would sit meditatively smoking, or walking up and down with a troubled face.

It was late in the afternoon, four days after, and Helen herself was out. Humphrey, alone in the studio, had been standing in the same reflective attitude for very many minutes, when he was roused by the sudden opening of the door, and Roger came in quickly.

"I'm afraid I ought not to bang in like this," he said. "But if you're not too busy, old fellow, I should like to talk to you a bit."

A curious look, as of a man who has taken a sudden and rather desperate resolution, and intends to carry it immediately into action, had come over Humphrey's face at the sight of his brother, and it intensified at Roger's words.

"Sit down, old boy," he said. "I've been wanting a talk, too."

Roger paused in the act of settling himself in his chair, and looked at him.

"You have?" he said. "Well, go ahead, then. Or wait a bit," he added. "Suppose I have my say first? It's rather on my mind."

"Go on, then."

But Roger did not go on. He leant forward in his chair, propped his chin on his hands, and his elbows on his knees, and sat staring into the fire.

"Humphrey, old boy," he began, at last, in a low voice, "there's no one knows so well as you do how hard I was hit."

Humphrey started, and looked down at him, his face full of sympathy and hope.

"Yes," he said.

"I shall think of her as long as I live, as — as — well, as altogether different to any other woman," Roger went on, slowly; "like a queen, or a saint, or something like that. But I'm only a man, you see; and a man wants something nearer to him for his wife, I've come to understand." He paused, and Humphrey's face changed suddenly; he turned it away without speaking, and, after a moment, Roger went on:

"I told her just how it was, and she understands exactly. I—she—we——" He paused again, having confused himself past all extrication, and Humphrey said, without looking at him:

"You are not talking of Selma, now. Tell me in so many words what you mean."

"I am engaged to Mervyn Ferris," answered Roger.

He never knew what it was that Humphrey had been going to say to him. When he asked, on a sudden thought as he said good-bye, Humphrey had forgotten.

CHAPTER II.

I⊤ was early in the afternoon of the following day, and Helen was hovering about in her drawing-room, glancing impatiently and incessantly at the clock. She had been obliged to go out early that morning without seeing her sister. Humphrey had told her, after Selma had gone to bed the night before, of his brother's engagement. She had seen that there was a letter in Mervyn's writing for Selma that morning, and she had hardly been able to restrain her impatience, when, on her return home, she had received a message to the effect that "Miss Selma said she was at work, and would be down about three o'clock."

"I do wish she would come," thought Helen

again, as she looked at the clock for the ninth time in the course of half an hour. " It is past three." And, as she glanced towards it, the door opened and Selma came in dressed for walking.

" Here you are at last ! " cried Helen. " Oh, are you going out ? " she added, disappointedly.

" I'm going to dine with the Tyrrells," returned Selma. " Miss Tyrrell asked me to go early."

Her voice was perhaps a shade thinner than usual, but perfectly soft and composed. Her face was shaded by her hat; but there was a colour in her cheeks, and her eyes were very bright.

" You — you had a letter this morning, didn't you ? " said Helen, and then she went suddenly round to Selma and took her tenderly into her arms. " Oh, my dear, I am so glad ! " she cried.

" I am glad, too, dear; very glad indeed."

"I know," returned Helen. "That's why I'm so delighted. Of course it's nice that Mervyn and Roger should be happy; but it's you I'm thinking of. Oh, I have so wanted you to know that it was coming. Did you see when they were here the other day? Of course you must have seen, though. Oh, Selma, I can't tell you what a relief this is to me for you, my poor dear! You can't reproach yourself any more when you know that he is happy. This will make all that trouble, dear, as if it had never been, almost, won't it?"

"Almost, Helen. Yes."

It was very significant of the gulf which lay between the Selma of two years ago and the Selma of to-day, that it seemed quite natural to Helen that her sister's words should be few and her manner quiet, pleased as she believed her to be. Selma was very seldom either demonstrative or impulsive now; never, indeed, except about something which touched her keen artistic sympathies; but the

change had settled upon her so gradually that
Helen had almost forgotten that she had ever
been different.

"It's funny that it should be Mervyn,
isn't it?" continued Helen, with an amused
laugh. "I rather thought Mervyn would never
marry, dear little thing. Sylvia says"—Helen
had been with Sylvia that morning—"Sylvia
says that they are so funny. They both declare
that it is because they both think there is no one
in the world like you! You've quite made the
match, Selma! I congratulate you, darling!"
And Helen kissed her sister again.

"Nobody hopes more heartily than I do that
it will be a very happy one," answered Selma,
moving as her sister released her, and walking
up to the window, putting on her gloves.

"Oh, must you go?" said Helen as she
saw what she was doing. "We haven't half
talked it over yet, and I've been longing so to
tell you all about it."

"I'm afraid I must," returned Selma. "I've

written to Mervyn, of course, but give her
my dear love if you see her before I do. Good-
bye for the present, dear."

It was a long drive from Humphrey
Cornish's house to the Tyrrells'; but the half-
hour that had passed was not long enough
to account for the change which had taken
place in Selma by the time she stood in Miss
Tyrrell's drawing-room. Her face looked—as
though some strain on the muscles had been
entirely relaxed — haggard, exhausted, almost
stupid; her eyes were hollow and dull, and
there was no colour even in her lips. There
was no one in the room, and, as she realised
the fact, she sank into a chair as though her
one desire was for absolute inaction, mental and
physical. She had no idea how long she
waited; she vaguely wondered whether she had
been asleep, when Miss Tyrrell eventually came
to her with profuse regrets for having kept
her waiting alone, and explanations of her apparent neglect.

"Now, dearest girl, let us make ourselves very comfortable," she said at last, "and let us have a nice little chat. I am going to be very serious indeed."

She spoke in her most winning and irresistible tone, and Selma, taking the chair she indicated, responded with a vague smile.

"But first of all, dear girl," continued Miss Tyrrell, "before I begin to scold, I must tell you how utterly charmed and touched I was at the last matinée! I was with Lady Drummond, Selma, and I assure you she was in ecstasies. It was admirably artistic."

Miss Tyrrell paused; but, rather to her surprise, there was a perceptible interval before Selma said, "I am glad."

She spoke strangely, more as if she were searching under some heavy oppression for the words which she vaguely felt she ought to say, than because she cared at all. Miss Tyrrell glanced at her sharply.

"Good gracious, child," she exclaimed most

inartistically, but quite naturally, "do you know
that you look quite plain?"

Selma did not answer—apparently she was
entirely indifferent on the subject—and, after
a horrified pause, Miss Tyrrell recovered herself
and her manner, and rearranging herself in a
new attitude, began, in a deliberate and solemn
voice :

"Selma, the time has come when I feel
it my duty to you as an artist to speak to
you most seriously. I had intended doing so
in any case, but the sadly palpable proofs in
your face of the truth of what I am going to
say make me even more anxious than I was
already." Miss Tyrrell paused, and looked
gracefully for her pocket-handkerchief that her
next words might be the more impressive. "I
have known for some time," she continued, with
the air of a seer, "I have said it to myself,
I have said it to John, I have said it to every
one : 'That dear girl is overworking herself;
she will lose her beauty, she will spoil her

career if something is not done!'" Miss
Tyrrell paused again, and this time Selma said,
languidly :

"I am not overworked, thank you."

"You must absolutely give yourself a rest,"
pursued Miss Tyrrell; "you must have a little
change ; you must go about and see people.
Dear girl, I think you cannot know how greatly
you have wounded me by refusing to come
and give me your help at our little 'at home'
on the second. How that party weighs upon
my mind," said Miss Tyrrell, in a plaintive
parenthesis, "tongue cannot tell. But it is
not for my sake, Selma, but for your own,
that I am most deeply anxious that you should
be here."

Selma put her hand wearily to her
head.

"You are so kind, dear Miss Tyrrell," she
said, and her voice was dull and toneless,
"you are most kind; but please don't ask
me."

"I do ask you," returned Miss Tyrrell, suavely. "It is your duty to yourself as an artist that is involved; your duty to your art itself. It is infinitely painful to me to see you throwing yourself away, dear girl. Will you not relieve me by promising to give yourself at least this one holiday? Come to me, dearest girl, come to me on the second."

With a sudden movement, as though she were hardly conscious of anything but physical pain, Selma rose to her feet.

"I will come," she said, faintly, "I will come. Miss Tyrrell, my head aches. May I——"

And then, before Miss Tyrrell could reach her, she had slipped to the ground, white and unconscious.

Selma did not play that night. Miss Tyrrell, triumphant, but feeling that so practical an endorsement of her words on Selma's part was more than she was prepared to cope with, sent for Helen, and late in the evening

Selma was taken home. She had been over-working herself absurdly, every one said, and all her strength, physical and mental, seemed to have given way at once. She lay all the next day, and for several days following, almost motionless, and though she was only absent from her work at the theatre for the one night, it was evident that she forced herself to fulfil her engagement simply from a sense of duty, with no spark of professional enthusiasm to help her. All the forthcoming matinées were postponed indefinitely, without a word of protest from her; she seemed to have not the faintest desire to resume any of the occupations at which she had worked so feverishly.

But she was young and strong, and in a few days she was going about the house, list-less and uninterested, but no longer actually ill. She had gone up to her own room one afternoon, and Helen, sitting alone in the drawing-room, was listening for the sound of

her piano, wishing she could hope that her
sister was either practising or studying.

"She doesn't seem to get right, as she
should," thought Helen, anxiously. "I wish
something would happen to rouse her. I don't
believe she will be well enough to go to the
Tyrrells' 'at home' to-morrow. I wish——"

But Helen's meditations were here cut
short. There was a ring at the front-door
bell, and a moment after, to her great delight, Sylvia Cornish and Mervyn Ferris came
in together

"Oh, I'm so glad to see you both," cried
Helen, eagerly. "Sylvia, that's a delicious
chair. Mervie, come and sit here. We'll have
some tea this minute."

The two girls had been shopping, and as
Helen settled them down in a cheery fuss—
she was a very newly-married Helen still, and
delighted to do the honours of her house—
Mervyn showed her a large bunch of lilies she
had in her hand.

"They are for Selma, Helen," she said. "Is she better?"

"We have been so sorry to hear of her illness," added Sylvia, in a very different tone of voice from the tone she would have used in speaking of Selma before Roger's engagement to Mervyn.

"She is better, thanks," answered Helen, with a grateful glance at Sylvia. "She will come down, I expect, when she knows you are here."

"She isn't working, is she?" said Mervyn. "Helen, do you think I might run up to her? I—I haven't seen her yet," she finished shyly, meaning thereby that, owing to Selma's illness, she had not seen her since her own engagement.

"Run up by all means," laughed Helen, and Mervyn departed hastily with her lilies, to reappear behind Selma, a little later, with very flushed cheeks and big bright eyes.

During the half-hour that followed their appearance in the drawing-room, Helen was delighted to see that Selma was far less languid, and had more colour in her cheeks and brighter eyes than she had had for days. A little change and society were decidedly good for her, Helen thought, and when Sylvia and Mervyn were gone, she said cheerfully, as Selma moved rather restlessly about the room :

"You will feel quite inclined to go to Miss Tyrrell's to-morrow, after all, I hope."

Selma came up to her and stood by her work-table, winding and unwinding a reel of cotton as she answered, as though her superfluous energy craved an outlet, however trivial.

"Shall I go?" she said, restlessly. "I may as well, perhaps."

"It will do you good," replied Helen, practically.

"Perhaps."

A triumphant conviction was borne in upon Helen that she had been a most sage adviser, when, some four hours after she had seen Selma

off to the "at home" the next afternoon, she
received a telegram to the effect that her sister
was stopping all night with Miss Tyrrell; and
her conviction would have been strengthened
if she could have seen Selma as she sat that
night, after the performance, with Miss Tyrrell
and her brother in Tyrrell's smoking-room. She
was sitting on the wide fender-stool, wearing
a tea-gown of Miss Tyrrell's, which, artistic as
it was and well as it suited her, made her look
strangely unlike herself, and perhaps gave her
the appearance she wore of being slightly posed
—a hitherto unheard-of condition with Selma.
Her face was flushed and eager, her eyes bright
and excited, and she talked and laughed with
a feverish little triumphant air, until Miss
Tyrrell exclaimed, delightedly :

"Dear girl, you look like another creature.
Doesn't she, John?"

"She looks like a very pretty creature,"
returned Tyrrell, looking Selma full in the face
as she turned to him with a little laugh.

The party had been a signal success; and its most brilliant feature, not artistically, but socially, had been Miss Selma Malet. To her dying day Miss Tyrrell asserted that the change that that afternoon had seen in her *protégée* was entirely owing to her own admirable reasoning; but whether or no such was the fact, the change itself was certainly no delusion. Selma had laughed and talked, allowed herself to be flattered and flirted with, and had apparently thoroughly enjoyed herself, as she had never done "in society" before.

All the afternoon, while she formed the centre figure of his party, Tyrrell had watched her in her new departure with distinct satisfaction, but with no surprise. He read her by the light he thought he had obtained in Humphrey Cornish's studio nearly three weeks before.

John Tyrrell was, before all else, a man of patience, and he had been playing a waiting game for nearly two years. There was nothing in life so interesting to him as success — the obvious, tangible wealth and social power for which the word stood in his vocabulary. He had known Selma Malet all her life, and the possibilities which lay open to the genius in her—genius which no man was more capable of appraising — had made her developement and introduction an interesting piece of brain-work to him. But he had considered her as a very perfect piece of mechanism with his intellectual faculties only, until about two years ago. It was on the afternoon when he first met her as the promised wife of another man that she first appeared to him in the light of a beautiful woman, and a desirable acquisition. Her beauty and charm had suddenly appealed to his senses; the social position which he knew might be hers whenever she should choose to take it, and which she would necessarily share with her husband — should that husband be himself—had gradually appealed to his ambition as a man of the world.

Two objects had formed slowly in his mind

after his meeting with her at the dance to which
she had gone with Mrs. Cornish and Sylvia
during Roger's absence in Liverpool, and he
had pursued them steadily and without haste
ever since.   He had broken off her engagement
with Roger Cornish, believing honestly that she
would be miserable in a life from which Art
must be for ever excluded ; but determined also
to make her eventually his own wife.   He had
given her, professionally, every chance and
advantage which it lay in his power to give,
because he looked upon every step she made
artistically as a step toward that which he
intended her to attain ; toward that which he
considered the most desirable thing modern
life has to offer—social notoriety.

Tyrrell was a man for whom the world had
been too much.   Early success — popularity,
money, social power—had been too much for
the spark of genius with which Nature had
endowed him.   If he had had to struggle in his
youth and early manhood ; if he had known

artistic success before his personal gifts had
brought him popularity; he would doubtless
have been what he had it in him to be—a great
artist. He had been flattered and overpaid
for what he knew to be superficial and accomplished without effort; he had given the
world what it asked and applauded, and he was
a society favourite. Perhaps the one point about
him still in his favour was the fact that he never
deceived himself. He had ceased to believe in
Art—in anything but tangible position and
wealth—and he used no phrases to himself
about the matter. There had been moments
in his intercourse with Selma as her master,
and later as her manager, when her simple,
single-minded devotion to her art had touched
him, had stirred the old artistic instinct in him,
in spite of himself. The Duchess's matinée had
been such a moment. He had caught fire then
at her enthusiasm, and had been for the time
being so carried away that the cynicism of
reaction in him was harder than ever. But his

professional work and his social work were, in his eyes, equally means to an end which he could have attained by neither singly ; each was a matter of business, and was regarded by him from no other point of view.

Until within the last twenty-four hours, both the ends he desired to accomplish with regard to Selma had seemed as far from him as they had been when he first laid his well-calculated plans for their attainment. He was no nearer making Selma his wife, and he was no nearer making Selma a social power, than he had been then. She had been so absolutely innocent and unconscious, that any attempt on his part at anything approaching love-making had fallen utterly flat. She had altogether refused to have anything to say to society.

The time had arrived now, however, when his desires, matrimonial and social, seemed to have come practically within his reach. He had hitherto been powerless against an impene-

trable something in Selma which prevented
his advancing one hair's-breadth. Try as he
would he could make no way against it, nor
could he define it; he was baffled on every
side by a sense that he was moving in the
dark. The light that had dawned upon him in
Humphrey Cornish's studio had, in his own
opinion, not only shown him the obstacles that
lay in his path, but had shown them to him
just at the crisis when they might most easily
be dealt with.

When he induced Selma to break off her
engagement, he had had not the faintest respect
for her feeling for Roger; he had looked upon
it as a girlish fancy which would assuredly
wear off with time. But now from what he
had seen in Selma's face as she watched Roger
Cornish and Mervyn Ferris in the studio, he
had deduced a theory that, with what he
mentally designated as the self-torturing instinct
of a thorough woman, she had dwelt on Roger's
unhappiness and her own imaginary sacrifice,

E 2

until she had magnified her girlish infatuation
into what she chose to consider a consuming
passion. These premises established—and in
Tyrrell's mind they were very firmly established
—Roger Cornish's new engagement could not
fail, Tyrrell argued, to bring about a state of
mind in her which would only need judicious
management to bring about both his objects.
Jealousy and despair, however fictitious, would
catch at any distraction, he calculated; the
excitements of society, judiciously presented to
her, would serve such a purpose well enough;
and, one season accomplished, the completion
of his social plans for her would be merely
the work of time. Wounded pride, he told
himself, would inevitably hurry her into marriage, and he had only to play his cards
well to ensure its hurrying her into marriage with himself. He looked at her now
as she sat there on the fender-stool, her new
self-consciousness sitting so gracefully upon
her as she laughed up into his face, and

taking the cigar from between his lips, he said, carelessly :

"It's almost a pity you refused the fancy dress ball, isn't it, Selma?"

"Do you think so?" she answered, lightly.

"Suppose you change your mind, dear girl," said Miss Tyrrell, eagerly. "John and I are going, of course, and I dare say I could arrange it with Lady Winslow. It will be a delightful evening."

"Exercise your privilege and change your mind, Selma," said Tyrrell, waving off the smoke of his cigar as he spoke. Selma hesitated, and then she turned to Tyrrell with a look on her face which he had never seen there before—a reckless look.

"Do you think it leads to anything?" she said, looking him in the eyes as if he and she were alone together, and speaking with a strange ring of demand in her voice. "Tell me!"

Tyrrell laid down his cigar and answered her slowly and deliberately, using the only argument which would, he knew, have any weight for her.

"I think that a good social position is the very greatest help towards the attaining of the highest artistic position. I think it is a help which no artist can afford to neglect."

There was another pause, and then Selma sprang to her feet.

"Take me to the fancy dress ball, dear Miss Tyrrell!" she cried; and her voice was as reckless as the look in her sparkling eyes. "Don't let me neglect anything that will help me, pray!"

A great deal of artistic advertising may be done in a very short space of time by a lady of Miss Tyrrell's peculiar talents; and, though there were only a few days to pass before the fancy dress ball in question, when the night arrived nearly every one in the room was talking about the expected appearance of Miss Selma Malet. The Tyrrells were late; all the other theatrical lions and lionesses had arrived

to roar unheeded, as quarter of an hour after
quarter of an hour slipped by, and still Miss
Selma Malet did not put in an appearance.
Her previous refusals of all invitations had been
utilised by Miss Tyrrell to the utmost. Everybody knew that Miss Selma Malet was wholly
devoted to her art; if she deigned to smile
now and then upon society, society understood
that it was to be deeply and humbly grateful,
and, being at the bottom a meek and credulous
institution, society was prepared to fall immediately upon its knees, and there remain
until a newer idol should be presented to it.

"What will she wear, I wonder?" said a
gallant of the court of Charles the Second, who
had worshipped Selma from the stalls for some
weeks, and was burning for an introduction.
"You know her, of course, Lady Latter?" he
added to the lady on whom he was bestowing
as much of his limited intelligence as he could
collect.

The two years which had gone by since

Lady Latter and Tyrrell had met at Mrs. Oliphant's had left her in looks and manner almost as they found her. She had been looking old last season, people had said; but this year she appeared to have completely recovered herself, and her dark, piquant face was only a shade harder and more daring for the time that had elapsed. She was slightly and very admirably "made up," and her dress, from the point of view either of originality or effectiveness, was perfect. If some people might have thought that, considered as clothing, it left something still to be desired, Lady Latter considered that half the point of a fancy dress lay in the superior facilities it offered, compared with ordinary evening dress, for sailing as near the wind as possible.

She nodded to an acquaintance across the room, as her companion spoke, and then turned to him with a laugh, which was not a pleasant one.

"Indeed I don't!" she said. "You forget

that this budding genius is altogether superior
to such an inferior being as I am! To tell
you the honest truth, too," she continued, with
an indescribable grimace, "these superior young
beauties bore me. They bore all the ugly
women in London, no doubt," with a quick
change of tone, and another laugh; "but I
am the only one who would own to it."

"You've seen her play?"

"Yes—for my sins! I saw her in that
dreary old fossil of a play Tyrrell dug up for
the Chinese business, and she and he together
nearly killed me with suppressed laughter. It
made one feel quite young and romantic to
see such an old stager as Tyrrell making such
a fool of himself. ' Bianca! oh, Bianca!'" she
quoted, striking an attitude—another privilege
attending fancy dress in Lady Latter's eyes—and
burlesquing Tyrrell's tone and manner. Then,
suddenly returning to her own natural demeanour,
she exclaimed, as nearly every one in the room
exclaimed at the same instant: "Here they are!"

Miss Tyrrell, dressed very perfectly as an Egyptian sorceress, was just presenting to her hostess a figure which looked as if it had stepped down from one of Romney's most charming canvases, it was so lovely, so gracious, so girlish. The dress was very simple and rather dark in colouring, relieved by the big white fichu. Selma wore no ornament of any kind, her own beauty was the dominating note in her appearance; and the whole effect against the mass of bright colour and gorgeous jewellery in the room was, as Miss Tyrrell had intended it should be, indescribably striking. Behind her, an admirable foil, was Tyrrell in a splendid dress of old Venice.

As far as Selma's success was concerned, Lady Winslow's fancy dress ball was a repetition of Miss Tyrrell's "at home" on a more extended scale. Everybody in the room who was "anybody" had been introduced to her, and she was talking and laughing with a lovely, excited flush on her cheeks, and with eyes like stars, when, about an hour after their arrival, Tyrrell made his way to her side.

"Oh, nobody else just yet, please!" she cried, with a little laugh which was as unlike the simple, natural Selma, as was the gesture with which she turned to him. "Breathing space, if you please, Mr. Tyrrell!"

"Breathing space by all means!" he answered; then with a sudden hardly perceptible change of manner, he said: "Ah! Lady Latter, how do you do?"

A movement of the crowd had suddenly brought them close together, and face to face, and she held out her hand to him, saying:

"I thought you had gone into retirement! We haven't met for ages!"

He made some conventional rejoinder, and as he spoke, as if accidentally and unconsciously, he drew a step or two off from where Selma and her court were standing. Lady Latter stopped him.

"Introduce your beauty, Tyrrell," she said, carelessly.

He hesitated.

"Introduce your beauty," she repeated, raising her voice a little, and looking him full in the face. He turned to Selma. She had apparently heard Lady Latter's words— Lady Latter's insolence was one of her sources of power—for her eyes were very girlish and indignant.

"Lady Latter wishes me to introduce you to her," said Tyrrell—"Miss Selma Malet— Lady Latter."

Miss Selma Malet acknowledged his words with the bow of a young princess, and at the same moment Lady Winslow came up to the group with a very distinguished peer by her side.

"Miss Malet!" she said, "may I introduce Lord Gildon? I hope he may persuade you to go down to supper. Mr. Tyrrell, why don't you take Lady Latter to have some supper?"

A moment later Selma had walked away

with her peer—she would have walked away
with any one from "that woman," as she
mentally designated Lady Latter—and Lady
Latter and Tyrrell were practically alone together.

"May I have the pleasure?" he said, without looking at her.

She put her hand on his arm in silence.

CHAPTER III.

It was a windy March morning, and Humphrey Cornish, alone in his studio, cast an anxious glance up at the dark sky, which was visible through his window. He cast an anxious glance, also, at the door, as though he expected some one, and then he returned to his contemplation of the canvas before which he was standing.

Nearly two years had passed since he had sketched for Selma those dresses for Pauline which she had never worn; but Humphrey was as little altered as was the room in which he stood. There were a few additional beauties about the room, in the shape of valuable artistic properties. Its owner was an A.R.A. now, and his financial difficulties were a thing of the past.

Humphrey's face was a little more thoughtful, a little more worn ; as he stood there looking at his picture, its expression was one of concentration, thought, and even of painful effort. But in spite of this, the impression conveyed curiously by both studio and painter was one of peace, of human thought and work at its finest and least demonstrative. The two years had passed quickly for Humphrey. Time was marked for him mainly by the work he did in it, and the work he did faded into insignificance in his eyes as soon as it was accomplished, and the work that lay before him took its place.

He was still looking at his picture when the opening of the door made him turn his head, and Helen came in.

"She will be down directly, dear!" she said.

It was a plumper, graver, more matronly Helen, to whom the two years past had been too full of experiences to allow of their seeming quick in the living or short in the looking back. The pretty blue eyes had lost their girlishness and were deeper and sweeter; her voice was fuller and older, and though she looked as happy as ever, it was the happiness of a woman, not of a girl. There was a little Helen upstairs, a very little Helen indeed, with brown eyes and bright curly hair, and Helen wondered now how she had ever thought herself happy without the gift those baby hands had brought her.

She came up to Humphrey and stood by his side looking, as he had been looking, at the picture.

"Have you much more to do?" she said. "It looks to me finished."

"Not much. I could do it in an hour or two."

"It always makes me feel as if I wanted to cry!" said Helen, looking at it as though she were trying to understand what it was that could have such a very unusual effect on her.

The subject of the picture was taken from

"Cymbeline," and there was only one figure
in it—Imogen, who had apparently just risen
from the rough stone by which she stood with
an open letter in her hand. The figure was
perfect in pose, the colouring and arrangement
exquisite ; but the power of the picture, the
power which went straight to Helen's woman-
liness and touched it as no mere beauty could
have done, lay in the face. The features were
Selma's—Selma's with the beauty of a noble
womanhood added to them—but the expression
was Imogen's. The eyes, which seemed to meet
the eyes of every one who looked at the picture,
were wide and dark with anguish, and the
beautiful lips were parted as if to speak. And
every line of the white, lovely face seemed to
radiate innocence and simple, womanly dignity
and grief.

"It is Selma's features that touch you,"
said Humphrey, quietly, studying his wife's
face as she looked at the picture. His work
on that picture had been his life for months

past, and he dared not trust the unconscious criticism which Helen's face conveyed. But Helen shook her head.

"No!" she said. "It's not that. I don't think it's quite so like Selma as it was. I mean she isn't quite like it, somehow." She paused a moment, looking into the pictured face. "She is so good," she said, softly, and sympathetically speaking of the pictured face, as though it were a living woman. "She is so good, and it's so dreadful for her."

She stood a moment longer and then turned away, and Humphrey said:

"It is getting very late, Nell."

"I know!" she said. "She is really coming. She says she was so late last night that she couldn't get up this morning. She sent a note down to the theatre instead of going to rehearsal. I'm so glad the sittings are over, Humphrey. She has been tiresome about them lately."

"You forget that it is very kind of her

to sit to me at all," remarked Humphrey, quietly.

Helen laughed. "I'm always forgetting all kinds of things about her," she said, and then her smile died out rather suddenly. "I feel as though I hardly knew her," she said, with a little sigh.

Humphrey made no answer; he was studying his picture again, but this time rather absently. A few minutes later the door was opened with a quick, imperious touch on the handle, and Selma came in.

Helen had said that she felt as though she hardly knew her sister, and it was not strange that she should feel so. Selma was so entirely and indescribably altered that only the features of the Selma of two years before seemed to be left. Her eyes were large and beautiful as ever, but the dreaming youthfulness was gone, and they were brilliant and eloquent with the brilliancy and eloquence which is conscious of its own effect; the lovely mouth

was lovely still—lovelier, some people thought,
for the new expression into which the girlish
curves had subsided. In her carriage, in her
every movement and gesture there was an added
something which separated the new Selma im-
measurably from the old, and the something
was perhaps a gain; if she were more self-
conscious, she was also more finished and perfect
in manner. But in her face, lovely as it was,
though the latent power had certainly developed,
there was as certainly something lost; the depth
and dignity of expression which should have
strengthened, in the course of that developement, had nearly disappeared. She was a little
thinner, and she was looking rather pale and
dark about the eyes this morning as if from
fatigue. Miss Selma Malet had been for nearly
two years one of "society's" most distinguished
ornaments, and there were times when her
physical strength was tried by her life.

"I'm late, Humphrey," she said, carelessly,
as she went up to the fire by which Helen

was sitting and held out to the blaze two
slender, delicate hands, on which were some
beautiful rings in these days. "I'm afraid
you've been waiting for me."

"I'm afraid you will be very glad to hear
that I shall not have to ask you for another
sitting," answered Humphrey.

"Really?" returned Selma; and then, as
a sound from upstairs called Helen out of the
room, she turned and moved idly to where
Humphrey was standing. "So she is nearly
finished," she said, looking critically at the
picture; "nearly finished. Are you under
the impression that you have painted — me,
Humphrey?"

She spoke the last pronoun with a curious
emphasis, proud, laughing, and serious, and she
looked at him as she spoke with an imperious
demand which was not all affected. The
picture was intended for the Academy, and
it had originated in a suggestion made towards
the close of the last season that Miss Malet's

portrait must be in next year's Exhibition.
The suggestion had been eagerly taken up
by two very fashionable portrait painters; but
Selma had said no to both of them. Humphrey
should paint her, she declared at home; Humphrey should paint her and become the fashion.
And Humphrey had smiled quietly and considered her attentively as he said:

"I am not a portrait painter, Selma."

Selma, however, was not accustomed to
having her word gainsaid, and she had apparently
set her heart on having her own way in this
case.

"Nonsense, Humphrey!" she said. "You
have painted me heaps of times. Paint me in
character if you like." And Humphrey, with his
artist eyes on the face and figure before him,
had stipulated that the picture must be painted
after his own fashion, and had asked her to sit to
him as Imogen—a subject he had long had in
his mind.

He looked at her now with the same

attentive, rather sad, expression on his face as
he said :

" Is it less like you than you expected ? "

" My dear Humphrey," she returned, with a
little laugh, "it's an admirable picture, and I
hope it will be a great success ; but really any
model would have answered the purpose quite as
well as I have done ; and one of the regular men
might as well have painted me, for any good
it will do you from that point of view. It isn't
in the least like me."

" What is the matter with it ? " he asked,
taking up his palette as she turned away and
walked to the raised daïs. She stopped and
looked back, first at the picture, and then into
a long looking-glass let into the wall, which
faced her as she stood. She was dressed in
Imogen's dress, and her beautiful hair, as it
fell about her, was the hair that Humphrey had
painted ; but these trifling points of similarity
and the superficial likeness of the features,
seemed to make the deeper contrast only sharper.

She stood a moment, looking from the glass to the picture and back again, and a faint colour came to her cheeks.

"You have painted a different woman," she said, and then she turned away again, and posed herself in silence. The silence lasted a long time. Humphrey worked on, growing every moment more absorbed, and something in the stillness, or the atmosphere of the place, seemed to depress Selma. She sighed a little, and moved restlessly.

"Are you tired?" said Humphrey.

"A little," she answered, absently. Then rousing herself, she said, quickly: "I beg your pardon, Humphrey. Did I fidget? Is that better?" There was another pause, and then she said: "I am afraid I have been troublesome about the sittings, Humphrey; but I am very sorry that this is the last."

"They have been more of a tie than you expected, I am afraid."

Selma laughed.

"That means, I suppose, that you could wish I had considered them more of a tie," she said. "Life is such a rush, Humphrey. Last season hardly seemed to have begun before it was over; the summer vanished before I knew the season had gone; and now it's March before I seem to be well settled into November. The last eighteen months have gone in a kind of flash."

She paused a moment, but Humphrey did not answer; and after a minute or two she went on, with another little laugh:

"There is no rush about you, Humphrey. You've no idea how quiet and peaceful you seem in here, or how soothing the sittings have been. I am very sorry this is the last," she repeated, with another sigh.

"Do you want soothing, Selma?"

"Well," she said, with a gaiety which was perhaps a little forced, "I am bound to say that I never feel the need except when I am undergoing the process. I become conscious then that

it is a very long time since I was not too busy
to think ; but, after all, what would one have?
One must go with the times ; and it is hardly
for me to quarrel with life, is it ? "

She turned to him as she spoke, regardless
of her pose in her brilliant consciousness of her
success, and instead of answering, he said,
quietly :

"Turn your head to the right, please." Then
as she obeyed with a quick, petulant movement,
"Thank you," he observed, and painted on in
silence, until she said, in quite a different tone
of voice :

"Do you want to keep me long to-day ? "

"How long can you give me ? "

Selma hesitated.

"There are some people coming to tea," she
said. "And I have to dress, you see. Will
another half-hour be enough ? "

"Quite enough, thank you. Don't wear yourself out, Selma, before the season fairly begins."

"And don't be late, Selma, this afternoon,"

said Helen, who had come into the room in time to hear Selma's last speech. "Last time you asked people to tea I had to talk to half-a-dozen friends of yours I didn't know at all for nearly half an hour, and we none of us enjoyed it."

"Selma's friends," as she called some three-score of Selma's society acquaintances indiscriminately, were something of a trial to Helen. She had vaguely understood last season that Selma was a great success; that she was always going out; that she knew everybody, and that everybody knew her; and she had taken a delighted pride in all her sister's proceedings. When Selma said carelessly that there were "some people" who would like to call, she had assented with alacrity, and was rather disappointed at first that Selma allowed so few visitors. "I can't have you overwhelmed, dear," she had said to Helen. And before very long Helen found the occasional afternoons, and the dozen or so of people who came to

them, quite as much as she cared for, unfailing
delight as it was to her to see Selma the
centre of attention. She never said as much,
even to herself; but she was conscious of a
secret antipathy to "Selma's friends," one and
all. "They make her seem so far away," she
said to herself.

In spite of Helen's words to her on the
subject of punctuality, several people had arrived
that afternoon before Selma came downstairs.
Helen was talking to Julian Heriot, who came
very occasionally to Selma's afternoons, and to
a lady as to whose name she was entirely in
the dark, and glancing with anxious eyes
towards the door, sorely divided between dread
of the appearance of more "people" and hope
of the appearance of Selma.

"My sister has been sitting to my husband
all the morning," she said, apologetically, as
her fears were realised and she had to receive
Nora Glynn, a pet aversion of hers. "She
will be here in a moment, I hope."

And then to her inexpressible relief the door opened again, and she subsided behind the tea-table as Selma's entrance took all further responsibility off her hands.

Selma was evidently quite accustomed and quite prepared to talk to half-a-dozen people at once — or rather to let them talk to her, for she did not exert herself in the least. She wore one of the frocks which were a constant source of admiration to Helen — a hybrid between fashion and art, in which she looked far more brilliantly beautiful than in the dress in which Humphrey had painted her as Imogen. Her self-possession, though it was the self-possession of self-consciousness now, was absolutely perfect.

During the next hour Helen's little drawing-room seemed full to overflowing, though there were never more than a dozen people at a time in it. They came by twos and threes; were polite even to the verge of patronage to the mistress of the house; laughed and

chatted with Selma, and went away again to
be replaced by others. Every one who came
knew every one else, every one who came was
easy and amiable with the consciousness that
it was an informal function to which many
who would have liked to come, did not come,
not being invited.

"How go the rehearsals, Miss Malet?" asked
Julian Heriot, as he brought her a cup of tea
in a temporary lull.

She took it from him with a smile of
thanks. "I am very glad to see you, Mr.
Heriot," she said. "I thought you did not
mean to come. Sit down and talk to me."

He did not take the chair her gesture
indicated, but stood looking down at her as
he said :

"Did I say I should not come? That was
very rude of me."

Selma laughed, a pretty, low, musical laugh,
which was as new in her as the expression of
her eyes as she looked up at him.

"You generally are rude, in a quiet, sarcastic way, don't you know?" she said. "One is so used to it from you. The rehearsals? Oh, they are dreadfully tiresome."

"Don't you like your part?" enquired Nora Glynn, who had just come up to say good-bye.

"It isn't a part," returned Selma, with a little shrug of her shoulders. "There's one scene with which I suppose I must try and do something, but really I haven't troubled much about it yet."

"You've been busy about your frocks, I suppose," said Miss Glynn, interestedly. "I hear they are wonderful. But what a trouble one has with them!"

Selma turned a serenely-surprised face upon the other. "I did not know you had a voice in the matter," she said. "I thought all your things were chosen by the management. Yes, my frocks are rather nice, I think, and I'm thankful to say they are nearly ready."

Nora Glynn had flushed angrily under Selma's eyes, and she held out her hand to say good-bye.

"I'm so glad," she said, recovering herself valiantly. "Oh, by-the-bye, have you heard what a success the girl in America has made with your part in 'Shadows'? I hear it is quite a hit. Isn't it extraordinary? I should have said there was nothing to be done with it! Good-bye, Mr. Heriot. Good-bye again, Miss Malet."

"Shadows" was the play which had run all through the last season at John Tyrrell's theatre. Miss Malet had failed to do anything in it but look like a vision of perfect beauty; it was a miserable part, every one had said.

As Nora Glynn turned away, Selma looked up at Heriot, with a calm little smile, and said:

"How she enjoyed telling me that! How she hates me!"

"You were rather hard on her," answered Heriot, laughing.

"Was I?" returned Selma, echoing his laugh. "Well, her airs are really insufferable, and either she gets worse or I get less tolerant. I am constantly obliged to try and extinguish her."

"If it is not too rude a thing to say, your words suggest the question: why does one meet her here?"

"Why? Ah, the reasons are feminine, Mr. Heriot, and I shall not attempt to translate them. But what about 'Shadows,' really? You don't mean to say that the Americans have extracted anything from Marie?"

Her voice was a little piqued under the laugh with which she spoke, and Heriot looked at her curiously as he said:

"It's a peculiarly American talent, isn't it, the talent for 'striking oil' in unexpected places?"

"But has she really?"

" So they say," he answered, carelessly.

Then there was another influx of people,
and Selma rose and went to receive them.
She was talking to the new-comers, and saying good-bye to some who were going away,
standing, laughing and talking, in the centre
of the group when the door opened again, and
a man came in alone. The servant's announcement fell unheeded. Helen was at the other
end of the room, and Selma's back was towards
the door. The new-comer was standing hesi-
tating, as though he had made a mistake,
when Selma turned, quite suddenly and un-
accountably, and saw him. With a little
gesture of apology she left the group of which
she was the centre, and went towards him, her
most brilliant, gracious, and self-possessed self.

"Ah, Roger," she said, "how do you do?
You will find Helen over there."

She had turned away again before he could
answer, and Roger Cornish crossed the room
to Helen.

"I didn't know you had a party," he said, in a low voice. "I'm awfully sorry, Helen."

"It's not a party," returned Helen, in the same tone, moving with him to the tea-table. "They are a few of Selma's friends. How is baby?"

"Very seedy," answered baby's father, despondently enough. "That's what I came to see you about, Helen. Mervyn wants you to go and see her to-morrow. She's dreadfully anxious, Helen."

Mervyn and Roger had been married very shortly after their engagement, and the tiny specimen of humanity, which was now nearly six months old, had been an anxiety for all his little life, and his very frailty seemed to make him the centre of the universe to his father and mother. Roger's tenderness for his little son, so like his tenderness for his little wife, was always half-amusing and half-pathetic to Helen, and she answered, cheerily:

G 2

"You are dreadfully anxious too, poor old boy. You are looking quite thin!"

Roger Cornish was certainly thinner; but his face was the better for it. The air of strength and capability which had always pervaded it, had grown with time, and his blue eyes were deeper and steadier, though they had lost nothing of their old simple directness. They were rather haggard to-day, and he smiled as Helen spoke; but before he had time to answer her, Selma, whose guests had nearly all departed, came up to the table with a late arrival—John Tyrrell.

"Give Mr. Tyrrell a nice cup of tea, Helen," she said. "He has come from the theatre, and he is tired. I take it for granted that you have come to scold me," turning to Tyrrell with a little laugh, as he shook hands with Helen; "and I wish to propitiate you."

"I'm glad you know you deserve to be scolded," he answered, lightly. "Why did you not come to the rehearsal?"

"Because I was otherwise occupied," returned Selma, daringly. "Oh, Roger, are you going? How is Mervyn? Not very strong! Oh, I am sorry. Give her my love, please; I wish I could make time to come and see her. Good-bye."

She shook hands with him, and then, as he and Helen left the room together, leaving her alone with Tyrrell, she turned to the latter, and said:

"Come and sit in this nice managerial-looking chair; I will bring you your tea, which is what I would do for no one else. Is anything wrong at the theatre? You don't look pleased."

"Your fancy, I assure you," he said, quickly, obeying her half-imperious, half-appealing mandate, and taking her cup from her hand. "Who would not be more than pleased in my place?"

Selma laughed, and turned away.

"I wish you wouldn't tease me so!" she

said, and then there was a pause and Tyrrell looked at her reflectively.

The two years that were gone had been to John Tyrrell on the whole as unsatisfactory as any two years he had ever spent. Two years ago he had prophesied within himself two things of Selma, reasoning from what he believed to be her feeling as to Roger Cornish and his engagement to Mervyn Ferris. He had prophesied, firstly, that she would be ready to marry any man who might offer himself; and, secondly, that she would throw herself, heart and soul, into a society life. As to his first theory, he had been obliged to own himself entirely in the wrong. Selma had not only shown no signs of desiring to marry, but she had shown very unmistakeable signs of intending not to marry; and Tyrrell had temporarily bowed to what he called the contrariety of women. But even this falsification of his first theory had not thrown him so entirely out in his calculations as had the

realisation of the second. Selma had taken
to a society life indeed, but she had taken to
it with a dash, and brilliancy, and a success
which seemed to carry her completely out of
his reach as she had never been before.
Tyrrell was far too keen to think of pitting
himself against the intoxicating rush and excitement of a first season—and such a first
season. He had stood aside, as it were, with
his most cynical smile, contenting himself with
the conviction that, though there were a dozen
men making love to her, she was far too deeply
absorbed in herself and her new position to
listen to any one of them. He was satisfied
to see that their old relations as master and
pupil never died out of her remembrance, and
that her manner to him, increasingly wilful and
imperious as it was, differed distinctly from her
manner to the rest of the world. The beautiful
Miss Malet became always Selma with him.

But with every month of restraint, with
every additional obstacle, his determination

to make her his wife had strengthened. Not only was the brilliant and popular woman of to-day infinitely better worth having than the girl of two years ago, but he had studied the position, and planned out his moves until his credit with himself as a diplomatist was at stake.

With the beginning of the second winter, he had come back to town thinking that now, when the first excitement was over for her, his first move must be made. But Tyrrell was not a man to risk a refusal in any case, and he knew, moreover, that the old friendly relations between them once broken, his game would be infinitely more difficult to play. For four months now, therefore, he had been feeling his way, and he was perfectly well aware that he had not even made a start. At every turn he was baffled by the very fact on which he had congratulated himself during the previous season, the fact that Selma never forgot that he was, as she had once called him, "her oldest friend."

As he sat now in the "managerial chair"
looking at the graceful figure turned away
from him towards the fire, he was deliberately
reviewing the position, and he moved slightly
as though recalling himself to the actual
moment as Selma said, lightly:

"Is there any news?"

She took a fire-screen from the mantelpiece,
and sat down in a low chair.

"Allison has sent in his notice."

"Really?" commented Selma, calmly, though
she coloured a little as he watched her.

The man alluded to had been a prominent
member of Tyrrell's company; a young man
who had come with honours from the Uni-
versity, and had been talked of as a very
rising young actor.

"He is going out to Australia."

"Really?"

"Don't you feel a little guilty, may I ask?"

Selma turned to him with a quick movement,
half petulant, half deprecating.

" I knew you were going to be angry with me about that very foolish young man," she exclaimed. " I think it's very unkind of you, Mr. Tyrrell. I couldn't tell that he would be so silly, and I couldn't accept him to prevent his going to Australia, I suppose. I dare say he'll get on very well in Australia."

"I'm not angry," answered Tyrrell, with a tone in his voice that Selma did not understand. " I've told you several times that I've no right to be angry with you—no more right than any other man."

Selma leant forward and smiled up into his face. "And I've told you as often that I give you the right," she said, imperiously. "You think I don't pay much attention to what you say; perhaps I don't. You think I'm spoilt; perhaps I am. But I like to think that there is some one who will tell me disagreeable truths still, though I know it's an odd taste. I like to remember that you knew me when I was little, and I don't think it's patient of you to give me up because I don't quite please you."

Tyrrell's cigarette-case was empty when he went to bed that night, and he had spent two hours in hard thought. Caution and patience have both their limits, and he believed that those limits were now reached. The first and essential point to be gained was that Selma should, without being startled or disturbed, be brought to think of him, however remotely, in the light of a possible lover. The idea must be suggested to her very gradually —so long as it was not suggested by himself, she might even smile at it if she liked, at first—but it must pervade her life little by little until it became as familiar to her as it was now undreamed of, as natural as the air she breathed.

When he left his study at last, the fire was out and he shivered slightly. But the policy of inaction had had its day, and his plan of campaign was arranged.

CHAPTER IV.

EASTER was over, and it was the day after
the production of the new play at Tyrrell's
theatre, for which Selma had been rehearsing
during Lent. Miss Tyrrell was lunching alone,
and enlivening her luncheon with a desultory
inspection of the criticism of the new piece
in the morning papers which Tyrrell, who
never took lunch, had just sent in to her
from his study. The piece had been a success,
and the notices, though not striking, were
favourable. Miss Tyrrell, having gleaned the
main points, found the detailed criticisms un-
interesting, and, having finished lunch, she was
idly re-reading the details given in one of the
papers as to the distinguished audience which

had been present, when the door opened and
Tyrrell came in.

"Are you ready, Sybilla?" he said. "There
is no hurry."

Miss Tyrrell, who had on her head an
arrangement of feathers, which she would have
described as a bonnet, put down her paper
and looked up at him.

"I'm quite ready when you are," she
replied. "We do not want to be there at
the beginning, though, I think."

The function to which Miss Tyrrell and
her brother were going together was a very
fashionable charity concert, at which Selma
was to recite, and as she stretched out her
hand for her gloves, which lay beside her on
the table, Miss Tyrrell said:

"Dear Selma seems to have made a
sensation last night. I hope she won't be
over-tired."

Tyrrell laughed. He was looking very
handsome and self-confident, and his fine

physique showed no traces of the hard work
the production of a piece always involved
for him. Tyrrell was far too practical and
keen a man to rely on his popularity to the
extent of neglecting his business, and his work
at the theatre during the last few weeks, though
it was no part of his social system to pose as
a hard-worked man, had been incessant and
severe. His voice had a hard, self-confident
ring as he answered:

"I think not. I don't think she has any
intention of over-exerting herself this afternoon,
unless she finds the congratulation she receives
exhausting. Every one will go round to the
artists' room this afternoon, no doubt."

"I had an idea that you thought she
would do nothing with the part?" observed
Miss Tyrrell.

"She did nothing with it at rehearsal, and
she did nothing but the one scene last night.
It was quite a sudden thing, and, by Jove,
how strong it was!"

"Dear girl, she will be more run after than ever," murmured Miss Tyrrell, as she rose. To her, as to Helen, though from widely different causes, Selma's popularity was a rather overwhelming spectacle. The "dear girl" was certainly no longer to be patronised.

The first part of the concert was nearly over when the Tyrrells arrived, and as they reached their seats, in the interval between two songs, a curious change, which she fondly hoped was a youthful blush, passed over Miss Tyrrell's artistic countenance.

"Dear me!" she exclaimed, in quite a fluttering voice, "isn't that Lord Ellingham next us? Yes, it is! Ah! Lord Ellingham, how do you do?"

Lord Ellingham was the same elderly and well - preserved gentleman as he had been when he assisted at Miss Tyrrell's tea-party so long ago, when the Duchess's matinée was first discussed. He had been a prominent member of artistic society for many years past; but in his youth and early manhood he had unfortunately found himself unable to concentrate his admiration of the beautiful as expressed in womanhood, and he was consequently still a bachelor. He was very well off, and it was dawning upon him that after a certain age the married state presents distinct advantages to man; with advancing years he was becoming an easy subject for delicate feminine diplomacy, and he responded to the charming smile bestowed upon him by Miss Tyrrell with an alacrity which warmed that lady's virgin heart.

"Fortune smiles on me," he remarked, gallantly.

Miss Tyrrell, after settling herself in her seat and zealously emulating Fortune, turned to her brother.

"Don't trouble about me, John," she said, sweetly. "You said you wanted to see Selma, didn't you? You will find me here if you like to come back for me."

"Very well," he answered, quickly. "Yes,

I am going round. Lord Ellingham, if I should not turn up again, you'll see my sister into a cab, I know." And with a gesture of farewell he turned away and disappeared.

If he had seen the look of comprehension with which Lord Ellingham followed him, he would have smiled as at the first sign of fruit from carefully scattered seed. Nearly a month had gone by since the night when Tyrrell had marked out his course of action; he had pursued it steadily ever since, and was beginning to look for results.

"Hallo, Brodie!" said Tyrrell, a minute or two later, as he turned into the passage leading into the artists' room; "what are you doing here?"

The man to whom he spoke, who was just in front of him, turned at the sound of his voice. He was a dramatic critic of a severe turn of mind, who was very rarely to be met behind the scenes.

"I want to speak to Duncan," he said,

bluntly, as he returned Tyrrell's greeting; "and I want to get away before your *protégée* makes a fool of herself."

"Who do you mean by my *protégée*?" returned Tyrrell, quietly. "If you are speaking of Miss Malet, my dear fellow, don't you think it's time the 'protégée' idea was exploded?" He paused a moment, and looked the other man full in the face with a great deal of meaning in his eyes, and then he said more lightly: "As to making a fool of herself, you are a sworn enemy to recitations, I know."

"I am," answered the other man, emphatically. "I am a sworn enemy to the depraving craving for something out of the common, which sends a fashionable audience into ecstasies over the recitation by Miss Malet of 'Twinkle, twinkle, little star,' or something equally soul-stirring. You can't see genius with a fool's-cap on every day of the week, consequently it's a bigger draw than genius in its native purple."

"You can't see the latter every day either, more's the pity," said Tyrrell, with a smile. "This is not the day of genius, Brodie!"

"It is not," returned the other, even more emphatically than before; "you're right, Tyrrell; and it's not the day for genius, either." He emphasized the altered preposition. "When such a phenomenon does happen to come along, nowadays, the chances are ten to one that society gets hold of it, and makes it— what it's making of Selma Malet. That girl has genius — I said so when she first came out — and it broke out last night again in spite of everything; but she'll be little better than a professional beauty in a year or two."

Mr. Brodie stopped, suddenly remembering the new impression Tyrrell had given him when he disclaimed what he called the "protégée" notion — the startling impression that Tyrrell had another relationship with Miss Malet in view—but before he could find words in which to apologise, Tyrrell clapped him lightly on the shoulder, saying :

"You're a cynic, my dear fellow, and you don't appreciate popularity."

They reached the door of the artists' room on the words, and, as Tyrrell opened it, the sudden light and confusion of voices, coming in sharp contrast to the darkness and quiet of the passage, made the two men pause for a moment. Then some one said, "Shut the door or they'll hear in the room," and Tyrrell shut it quickly and went up to Selma.

The room was nearly full. Half the musical and dramatic profession were helping in the programme in some capacity or other, and a good many people, artistic and literary, who were not there on business, had taken advantage of the informal nature of the arrangements to come round to the artists' room to exchange comments on the production of the night before at Tyrrell's theatre, and to congratulate Miss Malet on her last success.

Selma was standing in the middle of the room receiving congratulations on all sides, radiant, beautiful, and triumphant. She was talking to Julian Heriot at the moment, and she turned gaily to Tyrrell, holding out her hand as he said, in a voice and with a smile which seemed to more than one of those who gave way to him to take possession of her in an indefinable way: "You are not over-tired, I am glad to see!"

"Not in the least!" she answered, lightly. "Ah, Mr. Brodie, have you come to say something kind to me?"

She offered him her hand as she spoke with a smile that few men could have resisted, and Mr. Brodie looked at her for a moment with something in his keen eyes which was almost like pity.

"You wouldn't thank me for real kindness!" he said, rather grimly.

"That's what people say when they mean something too horrid!" cried Selma. "Did I do so badly last night?" she asked, with the laughing challenge of unassailable success.

"You did a great deal too well," was the answer. "But you did it in spite of yourself, and you would have done it better two years ago, if you will pardon my bluntness!" Mr. Brodie moved away with a slight bow as she turned to Tyrrell and Julian Heriot.

"Brodie revels in sardonic enigmas. If you've seen his notice of you in this morning's paper, Miss Malet," said Heriot, looking at her curiously, "you must know that he is consoling himself for the acute pain it is to him to praise." He paused a moment as she laughed merrily, with another keen look at her, wondering whether the truth of Mr. Brodie's just uttered words and the undertone of his published and more flattering criticism were really alike utterly unperceived by her, and then he said: "Well, I've no business here, I suppose, and I've a great deal of business elsewhere. That's painfully prompt,

Miss Malet!" he added, as Selma instantly offered to shake hands with him.

"I'm setting you a good example!" she said, laughing. "You said when you came in that you hadn't a minute to spare, and you've been here half an hour. Good-bye, Mr. Heriot!"

"Good-bye, Miss Malet!" he responded, and with a gesture of farewell to Tyrrell he left the room.

Selma was turning to speak to a famous soprano, who had just come in, when Tyrrell stopped her.

"Come and sit down, Selma," he said, in a low voice, "I want to speak to you."

He drew her away from every one, made her sit down and stood over her, bending down now and then as he talked, obliging her by his attitude to look up at him. His words were all about business connected with the theatre, but they were inaudible to the rest of the room, and, by the time it came to her turn to recite, more than one glance had been directed towards them and more than one pair of eyebrows had been slightly elevated. He waited while she was on the platform, and when she came off, amid tumultuous applause after giving a recitation little more artistic than that foretold by Mr. Brodie, he said, in a voice which was audible to several people :

"Is your sister coming for you or may I take you home?" He had never suggested such a thing before; but Selma, flushed, laughing, and excited after any number of rapturous "calls," did not notice.

"Helen is coming," she said. "I expect she is waiting. Will somebody please find my cloak?"

There was an instantaneous rush in search of it, and when it appeared Tyrrell took it calmly from the indignant young man who was bearing it proudly on his arm, put it on for her, and, apparently quite unconscious of the expression — or rather expressions, for they were numerous and conflicting — on the countenance of the defrauded one, took her away as one whose right it was to do so.

The action, trivial as it was in itself, was made significant by his manner, and it came as a climax on the impression that their previous tête-à-tête had made. As they disappeared, there was a moment's silence in the room, and then Nora Glynn's hard little voice made itself heard.

"It seems to me," she said, significantly, as she turned to the looking-glass to touch herself up preparatory to going on the platform, "it seems to me that we are all going to have a surprise."

John Tyrrell had not studied the follies or foibles of mankind in general, and London society in particular, for five-and-twenty years in vain. He had created the impression he intended to create, and as the season progressed he kept it cleverly before his world, never forcing it, never hurrying it, but never letting it die out. But the cleverest and most admirably calculated scheme can be helped on in its developement by all kinds of unconsidered trifles; and about a month after the concert Tyrrell's plans were materially advanced by a small being, of whose existence he was hardly aware—the little brown-eyed Helen.

It was an afternoon late in April, and Helen and Selma were standing on the landing outside the nursery door, the latter dressed— and very elaborately dressed — for walking. Helen's usually bright face looked as though she were being torn by conflicting emotions; but she shook her head decidedly.

"I couldn't bear to leave her," she said. "Of course I'm dreadfully disappointed because of Imogen; but it would be worse to be thinking about her all the time."

It was the day of the private view of the Royal Academy. Humphrey's picture had been hung in an excellent place; it had made

a great sensation among his brother painters ; at
the press view there had been rumours abroad
that it would be the most prominent picture
of the year; and under these circumstances
Selma had insisted that Helen should go with
her to the private view instead of leaving
her to go with Miss Tyrrell. Tyrrell, hearing
of the arrangement, and hearing also that
no known force would succeed in dragging
Humphrey to such a function, had suggested
that he should call and go with them ; and
though he had never done such a thing before,
and Selma told him laughingly that he was
only anxious to be at hand to keep her in
order, she had agreed to it as a delightful
arrangement. And now the afternoon had
arrived, Tyrrell was waiting in the drawing-
room, and little Helen had a little cold.
Helen herself, between her wifely pride and
her motherly anxiety, had been nearly torn
in two. But little Helen had won the day,
as had been inevitable from the first, and

her mother laid her hand once more on the nursery door, as she said :

"Go down, dear! Mr. Tyrrell has been waiting ever so long."

"Mr. Tyrrell can wait!" answered Selma, lightly. "Oh, I am so sorry, Nell. Is she asleep?" with a little gesture towards the nursery. "May I come in and look at her?"

"Come quietly," said Helen. She opened the door very softly as she spoke, and they went in together, and stood by the little cot which held half Helen's world. The brown eyes were shut now, the breath was coming softly and easily, and the little face was flushed with sleep. A little dimpled fist lay clenched on the pillow, and as Helen stood by with all the disappointment gone from her face, Selma, after standing for a moment looking down at her small niece, suddenly stooped and lifted the little fingers very tenderly to her beautiful lips. Then she

turned away and kissed her sister little less
tenderly.

"Good-bye, dear," she said, "I shan't pity
you."

A minute or two later she had passed
quickly downstairs, and had opened the drawing-room door.

"I'm afraid you've been waiting," she
said, as Tyrrell came forward to meet her.
"We shall have to go without Helen, I'm
sorry to say. My niece—I don't believe you
knew I was an aunt—has a cold in her tiny
head."

"I did know it," returned Tyrrell; "it's
a very proud position—for your niece." He
paused a moment as Selma turned away with
a laughing, petulant gesture. She always took
such speeches from him as sarcastic reflections
on the homage she received. Then he said,
slowly: "Mrs. Cornish cannot go with us?
Then, we go alone?"

Selma turned to him with a laugh.

"Obviously, Mr. Tyrrell; shall we quarrel, do you think?"

"I think not," he returned, looking at her, quietly.

"Then we had better start," she said, with her attention concentrated on the glove she was buttoning. "I want to see Imogen, and there will be no seeing anything in another half - hour. You look very thoughtful," she added, as she lifted her head and met his eyes. "Are you angry with poor little Helen?"

"No," returned Tyrrell, quietly, as he opened the door for her; "I am not at all angry with poor little Helen."

His feelings towards that small and unconscious assistant were cordiality itself when they arrived at Burlington House.

It was early in the afternoon; the rooms were hardly filled, and people were on the look-out for the appearance of celebrities of all kinds. Selma's entrance would, in any case, have been one of the events of the

afternoon, and before they had passed through
the first room, Tyrrell was aware that his
well - satisfied anticipations were more than
realised. The sensation produced by their
arrival together was immense. Selma herself
was, perhaps, the only person in the room
who was entirely unconscious of and untouched
by it. She had not been for two seasons in
society for nothing; she would have understood the position quickly enough if any
other man had been concerned. But with
Tyrrell, old habit was stronger than her new
perceptions. That any one should look upon
him in any other light than that of her
"oldest friend" simply never entered into her
head. She would have walked about with
him all the afternoon if he, thinking it better
to content himself with their entrance, and
with the fact that they were met in the
first room by two of the greatest gossips in
London, had not looked up his sister and
quietly contrived that she should be seen

with them on and off all through the afternoon.

"Give my love to poor little Helen," he
said to Selma, as he put her into a hansom.
"Are you coming with us to the Stanhopes'
to-night?"

"No," she said, "I refused. I——" but
the policeman, who was presiding over the
departures from Burlington House, did not
wait for her explanation, and she was driven
away.

It was a large "at home" to which Tyrrell
had referred, and when he arrived alone with
his sister that night, there was more than
one murmured exclamation of disappointment.
Nearly all the people in the room had been
to the private view, and were eager to see
further developements of the romance which
had been whispered about for weeks, and
which had assumed such solid proportions in
the eyes of society that afternoon. Everybody
was talking of Humphrey Cornish's picture of

Miss Malet, and everybody had something in-definite to add about Miss Malet and Mr. Tyrrell.

Miss Tyrrell was beginning to wonder why every one looked at her with the same enquiring smile as they spoke of the Imogen picture. She had early established it as a principle that all the credit of Selma's success was due to her, Miss Tyrrell, and that consequently admiration of Selma was subtle homage to her discoverer; but she thought to-night that that particular form of homage was rather overdone. She had a little private disappointment, too, of her own, and she was feeling languidly bored when she suddenly revived to a marvellously artistic interest in life in general, and in the elderly gentleman who was approaching her with the jaunty alacrity of early youth in particular.

"How do you do, Lord Ellingham?" she said. "I had no idea you were here."

Lord Ellingham had just come up from

the supper-room, where he had spent the last half-hour with an elderly and unamiable dowager, and he responded eagerly to Miss Tyrrell's graceful and gracious reception. She was very amiable, and she did not look elderly.

"You were not at the private view," she said. "That was very wrong. I consider it such a duty to make myself acquainted with the progress of Art in one's own country, though the progress, alas! is small enough."

"I agree with you," answered Lord Ellingham, promptly — he could have found it in his susceptible heart to disagree with nothing so insinuatingly enunciated by a lady—"I agree with you. I was not there, unfortunately, but I have heard all about it." Lord Ellingham spoke with what Miss Tyrrell mentally and very ungrammatically designated as "everybody else's exasperating smile." As a matter of fact, the only thing he had heard about the private view was the interesting statement that Miss Malet and Mr. Tyrrell had been there alone together; and he continued: "Is Miss Malet here to-night? I hear her portrait is the picture of the year. I hear, too," he added, with a meaning smile, producing one of the many details as to John Tyrrell's intentions, which society had been busily employed all the evening in fabricating, "I also hear that Tyrrell has bought it."

"That my brother has bought the Imogen!" exclaimed Miss Tyrrell. "My dear Lord Ellingham, what an idea!"

"Is it so unlikely?" answered Lord Ellingham, with another smile, and then Miss Tyrrell caught his eye, and a flood of light rushed in upon her. It brought with it such a sudden revelation, and the dreadful probability of the idea suggested to her became so instantly apparent that it absolutely took away her breath. What was to society rather a joke, was to the present mistress of John Tyrrell's house little less than a thunderbolt, and Lord Ellingham's fate was sealed on the instant.

"It seems to me unlikely," was what she said, suavely enough. "An actor, my dear Lord Ellingham, is unfortunately not a millionaire. It is hardly one of the pictures with which I should like to live. A little crude, I consider it."

"I wish we could compare notes on the subject," answered Lord Ellingham. "Have you been in the conservatory this evening? It is really very charming. Ah, there are your brother and Lady Latter," he added, as he moved away with Miss Tyrrell to be charmed by the effect of coloured lamps and palms, bowing as he spoke to Lady Latter.

Lady Latter returned his bow and then turned again to Tyrrell. They were standing together at the end of the room, he leaning up against the wall in a careless characteristic attitude, she playing with a large feather fan. They were carrying on a conversation in tones little lower than usual. The room

was crowded, and yet as she looked for a
moment straight into his eyes, something
seemed to rise round them and shut them
off alone together in a solitude which nothing
could destroy. She turned her head away
again immediately, unfurling her fan lightly
as she did so, and there was something in
her eyes, something which dominated their usual
insolent audacity, which made the careless tone
in which she spoke almost horrible by force of
contrast.

"Who would have accused you of being
so commonplace?" she said.

"I am happy to say that no one has
ever accused me of eccentricity!" returned
Tyrrell; his voice was as imperturbable as
was his handsome face.

"Is the position as comfortable and dignified
as it looks?" she asked, with a laugh.

"I beg your pardon?"

"The position of 'follower' to a fashionable
beauty! It is a new part for you—generally

cast to younger men or to old fools. I hope you are enjoying it?"

"May I ask by whom I am 'cast' as you say for the part in question, and who is the heroine of the romance?" enquired Tyrrell, calmly.

Lady Latter shot a quick glance at him and bit her lip.

"What innocence!" she said. "Well, you have educated your *protégée* to some purpose; and you are in good company! She has been talked about with nearly every man in London worth mentioning in the course of her three seasons."

For one instant, there was a gleam in Tyrrell's eyes as he turned his head slowly towards her which boded Lady Latter no good. But, as he looked at her, his intention apparently altered, and he looked away as indifferently as before, bowing to some one on the other side of the room. Lady Latter seemed to be losing her self-control; the laugh with which she had finished her speech was harsh and unpleasant, and her eyes sparkled evilly.

"I have never heard that solid foundations were a requisite of society gossip!" said Tyrrell.

"You were taking unnecessary trouble to provide it with solid foundations this afternoon, then," returned Lady Latter, with another laugh. "Or, perhaps you think that the *protégée* fiction is all - protective. It is a pretty fiction, and useful, I have heard." She was still moving her fan carelessly to and fro, but all her self-command seemed to be concentrated in her preservation of her negligent attitude. She looked with glittering, unseeing eyes at Julian Heriot in the distance to whom she should have bowed, and her words came rapidly and recklessly as though she hardly knew what she said. Tyrrell looked at her again, and his eyes were very calculating and very hard.

"Had you not better recognise Heriot?" he said, quietly. "What has he done that you should cut him?"

She paused a moment, and then, as she faced him with her dark face, darker than ever with impotent rage, he said, slowly and deliberately: "Of the protective capacities of useful fictions no one is better calculated to judge than Lady Latter. I am afraid I am monopolising your attention!"

He bowed slightly and turned away.

It was a fairly long drive home for John Tyrrell and his sister that night, but not a word was spoken by either on the way. Each appeared to have something to think of.

CHAPTER V.

THE subjects which occupied Miss Tyrrell's mind during her drive home were, apparently, sufficiently serious to deprive her of her night's rest, for she did not appear at breakfast the next morning. Her presence was not in the least necessary to her brother's comfort, and he was serenely absorbed in the morning paper, when he was interrupted by a knock at the door, and the servant who acted, on occasion, as Miss Tyrrell's maid, came in.

"If you please, sir," she said, "Miss Tyrrell wishes me to say that she is taking breakfast in her room, and she wishes to see you before you go out this morning if you will let her know what time."

"Let her know at what time I am going out?" asked Tyrrell.

"If you please, sir."

"I shall be in the study until twelve o'clock, tell your mistress. She can send for me, of course," said Tyrrell, returning to his paper as the woman answered "Yes, sir," and left the room.

As Tyrrell glanced down the column of the newspaper there was a smile on his face, which was not called up by the political leader he was reading. He was by no means unprepared for an interview with his sister, and it spoke well for the progress of his plans that she should demand it.

"I thought so," he said to himself. "Poor Sybilla! It's a blow for her!"

But the expression on his face was less sympathetic than amused, and the smile still touched the corners of his mouth as he finally gathered up his letters and departed to his study. An hour and more had passed, and he was lazily wondering whether his sister had reconsidered the position, and intended, after all, to fortify herself with further observation before she spoke, when he heard her step in the passage, and the next moment she opened the door.

"Good morning," he said. "Why did you not let me know you were down?"

"I thought I would come to you here," answered Miss Tyrrell; "you are not busy, John?"

"Not particularly," he said. "Come in." And, as she shut the door and sank gracefully into a chair, he pushed his own chair round slightly as he sat at his writing-table — his letters had been finished some time ago, and he was smoking a cigar—and waited to hear what she had to say, with the same little smile of amusement on his lips. Miss Tyrrell apparently found his expectant attitude rather confusing, for there was a moment's pause before she spoke.

"It is quite unnecessary, I am sure," she began, "that I should tell you how deeply I am interested in dear Selma."

As there was no one present to be impressed with the information, Tyrrell thought that, on the whole, it was unnecessary; but he only made a little gesture of assent, and waited for her to proceed.

"The poor dear girl has been a great deal talked about," continued Miss Tyrrell, with a sigh. "I am sure I only wish I could persuade myself that she has never given occasion for talk; but if she is careless, John, her friends cannot be too careful for her."

Miss Tyrrell paused solemnly, and her brother, with an irrepressible gleam of humour in his eyes, responded:

"Very true."

"Of course we both know, you and I, that you have known her since she was a little child, and that she looks up to you as to a guardian, and, equally of course, we know that you are not likely to fall in love like a boy, John; but we cannot expect the world to consider these things," said Miss Tyrrell, with a sigh of gentle superiority to the world and its ways, and a glance at her brother's unmoved countenance. "When once people have talked — especially if it is not for the first time — there are sure to be unpleasant things said when the talk comes to nothing."

Tyrrell knocked the ash from his cigar, and held it suspended between his fingers as he looked his sister quietly in the face. She had not explained herself, and he knew it; but it suited him to understand her. He preferred to come to the point at once.

"If you mean that people are 'talking,' as you say, about Selma and myself," he said, "I have no intention that such 'talk' should come to nothing!"

"Do you mean to say that you are thinking of marrying?"

Miss Tyrrell's surprise was well acted; she had had plenty of practice on the social stage. She had no doubt whatever that her brother meant to marry Selma; but the knowledge was not at all to her liking, though it was not so unendurably bitter as it might have been. She would thoroughly have enjoyed an attempt at giving her brother a very bad quarter of an hour, if, for reasons of her own, she had not thought it more prudent to content herself with the administration of stings of an intangible nature. She was no match for Tyrrell's keenness of observation, however, and he looked at her quickly, as it occurred to him that she was taking it better than he had expected.

"Yes," he said; "I am."

"You propose to marry Selma Malet!"

"I propose to marry Selma Malet," was the placid response, as Tyrrell put his cigar to his lips again.

There was a moment's pause, and Tyrrell

wondered whether his sister contemplated hysterics. "It could be done artistically," he told himself, with a grim smile. He was immensely surprised, and, being human, considerably relieved when she said:

"Am I to understand that it is settled?"

Tyrrell looked at her again in growing surprise. She spoke as though she were thinking of something else, and, instead of the hysterical symptoms he expected to see, he noticed that Miss Tyrrell looked nervous.

"It is not settled with Selma, if you mean that," he answered. "I don't want that to get about. There is plenty of time."

There was another pause, and Miss Tyrrell looked helplessly round the room.

"I — I'm sure I hope it will turn out well, John," she murmured, vaguely, and John Tyrrell, thoroughly puzzled, rose.

"I hope so, too," he answered. "It's time I went down to the theatre. This

was what you wanted to see me about, I
suppose?"

Miss Tyrrell clutched her pocket-handkerchief, and rose likewise. It was quite
impossible to come to the real point of the
interview, she felt, with "John" standing
over her like that. Miss Tyrrell was two
years older than her brother; and, though
this painful fact was shrouded in mystery
from the world in general, naturally he knew
it, and naturally she knew that he knew
it — that he knew also that he himself was
forty-seven, and that he was not incapable
of working a sum in simple addition. These
facts, coupled with such knowledge of her
brother's character as she possessed, rendered
the intelligence she wished to convey to him
a little delicate in her eyes.

"I have — there is another little point,"
she murmured, looking coyly at her hand-
kerchief. Such is the force of imagination
that there was a faint, wintry colour in her

cheeks; and, as Tyrrell looked at her, an idea dawned upon him. It was such an exquisitely ludicrous idea in his eyes, that its first effect was to make him bite his lip sharply to keep himself from laughing aloud. And then his face grew suddenly hard and stern.

"She's such a fool," he said to himself. "It may be any one." Aloud, he said interrogatively : "Yes ?"

"It's really a very trying thing to tell you, John," fluttered Miss Tyrrell, plaintively. "Especially if you will stand up. But, under the circumstances, I'm sure you can't help feeling for us."

"Us!" repeated her brother, with no trace whatever of the sympathy thus touchingly demanded in his voice. "Who is the other ? "

Miss Tyrrell clasped her hands gratefully.

"Now that is very kind of you," she said, quite forgetting, in her agitation, that there was no audience, and speaking in her most artistic voice, "to help me out so nicely. He—it—it is Lord Ellingham, John."

Miss Tyrrell at this stage was quite overcome with maiden confusion, and, in spite of "John's" erectness, she sank in artistic folds upon the chair from which she had just risen. She missed the expression on her brother's face: which was a pity, for it was a sight to be seen.

"Lord Ellingham," he said. And then, reflecting that, as he said to himself, it might have been worse, his sense of humour asserted itself, and he said: "You haven't told me why I am to sympathise with you and Lord Ellingham, Sybilla?"

A delicate tremor convulsed his agitated victim, and she murmured faintly:

"We are engaged."

Tyrrell always congratulated himself as upon his greatest artistic achievement that he did not laugh aloud. He contemplated his sister for a moment before he observed, adapting some words she had used to him earlier in their interview:

"I should hardly have expected you to fall in love like a girl."

Miss Tyrrell, who had regretted the words on which this comment was founded as soon as she had uttered them, stretched out a deprecating hand.

"We cannot account for these things," she said. "Dear Lord Ellingham has been most devoted, and I have not a heart of stone."

There was a suggestion of gurgle about her voice that warned Tyrrell that he would be wise to withdraw.

"Certainly not," he replied, promptly, and with commendable gravity; "Lord Ellingham is an excellent choice, Sybilla. You'd better ask him to dinner." And Tyrrell departed to the theatre, leaving Lord Ellingham's betrothed in possession of the field.

John Tyrrell's reflections on the engaged

couple during the day were complimentary
to neither lady nor gentleman. Miss Tyrrell
had a little money of her own, so that her
brother's marriage would have made no material
difference to her, and to marry Lord Ellingham,
either for his own sake or for the sake of his
position, seemed to Tyrrell an incredibly foolish
performance. There was nothing definite, however, to be said against the match. That the
lady was forty-nine, and the gentleman at least
ten years older, were facts to which no one was
prepared to swear, and which, after all, concerned
themselves alone. And from the point of view
of Tyrrell's own schemes with regard to Selma,
his sister, self-absorbed and complaisant, was
much more agreeable to contemplate than his
sister jealous, injured, and spiteful, as he had
calculated on finding her. Nothing that could
be used by him to his own ends ever escaped
Tyrrell's attention, and he took instant advantage of the fact that, under the circumstances, Miss Tyrrell might be used by him as

a valuable ally. Consequently, a fortnight after
the engagement with Lord Ellingham was
formally announced, Selma received a tenderly
pressing invitation from the bride-elect to spend
a week or so at her house, or, rather, at
Tyrrell's house.

"Ask Selma to stay here," Tyrrell had said.
"And Sybilla," he had added, in a tone which his
sister never disobeyed, "say nothing to her, you
understand."

Tyrrell did not intend that Selma's first
thoughts of him as her lover should spring up
under his sister's fostering care.

"Do you think of going?" asked Helen,
when Selma told her of the invitation, which
had been bestowed upon her by Miss Tyrrell
at a dance the night before with an air of
spontaneous cordiality delightful to behold.

The sisters were together in the dining-
room as Helen asked the question, and Selma,
who was standing at the open window in the
bright May sunshine, answered carelessly :

"Yes; I go out with them so much, you see. Besides," added she, with a little irrepressible smile, "I dare say poor Miss Tyrrell wants some one to talk to about her trousseau. The wedding is to be next month."

Helen's eloquence on the subject of Miss Tyrrell's engagement was unusually flowing. She considered it, as she expressed it, "Perfectly dreadful to see a woman make herself so ridiculous." But on this occasion she continued her needlework in abstracted silence, and Selma, rather surprised, went on affectionately:

"I shan't go until after the twentieth, Nell" —the twentieth of May was Helen's birthday— "are you thinking of that? Oh, Nell, what's the matter?" she finished, moving swiftly across the room to kneel down by her sister's side with both her beautiful arms round her, as Helen first lifted a pair of tearful blue eyes to her, and then wiped them hastily with an air which seemed to assert aggressively that she had not been crying.

"What is it, darling?" repeated Selma, tenderly, lifting to her a face which Miss Malet's admirers would hardly have recognised.

"It's very silly to cry," said Helen—this was indeed one of the first principles of her simple philosophy. "It's Mervyn's baby, dear; it's dying, poor mite, and I can't help thinking how I should feel if—if—oh, poor little Mervyn!" And if it was silly to cry, Helen was very silly indeed for the next few minutes; she leant her cheek against Selma's dark hair, and her bright pitiful tears came thick and fast as she thought of her own little Helen asleep upstairs. Selma held her very close, but there were no tears in her eyes. They were bright and rather wide, and she was very pale.

"Poor little Mervyn!" she repeated very low. "Has it grown suddenly worse, then?"

"Yes!" answered Helen, forgetting that she had thought Selma almost unconscious of the small Roger's very existence. "Roger came in last night.　Oh, poor fellow, he's heart-broken!"

Selma rose suddenly, her eyes brighter than before, with a look on her face as though she were keeping something at bay.

"Babies get better so wonderfully, don't they?" she said.　"Perhaps they are over-anxious, Helen.　Dear, I can't bear to see you cry."　She touched her sister's hair tenderly as she spoke, and Helen dried her eyes and looked up at her fondly.　It wasn't to be expected, she thought, that Selma should understand as she herself did.

"It is silly!" she said, answering her last words.　"I think I'll go and see if little Helen is awake and bring her down."

The little suffering life of Mervyn's baby came to an end that night, and Helen, when she told her sister with many sympathetic tears, was disappointed that Selma, though she was very sweet and comforting to Helen herself, seemed to be more occupied with an unsuccess ful evening frock than with Mervyn's and Roger's grief. Selma's engagements grew more numerous every day as the season advanced, and during the week that followed her sister hardly saw her; she was always either just going to a party, or just going to pay some calls, or just going to the theatre. And the few moments for which she was to be seen each day gave Helen the impression that she was doing more than was good for her, her eyes were so bright and feverish, and her manner so restless and excited.

"Don't overwork yourself," Helen said, when the day arrived on which Selma had arranged to go to Miss Tyrrell for a week, and she stood on the doorstep to see her sister into the hansom. "Take care of yourself, dear."

"Take care of yourself," returned Selma, gaily, as she kissed her. "And take care of my niece, Nell. Good-bye!" She sprang quickly into the cab and was driven away.

Selma had no luggage with her. She had sent it on in the morning, declaring that it would make her feel as though she were going away for months, if she drove off in state with a portmanteau. She had driven some distance—almost to the Tyrrells' house — with an absorbed, set expression in her eyes as though she were battling with pain of some description, when a sudden determination seemed to take possession of her; her pale face changed and flushed suddenly, she lifted her head impulsively, and stopped the driver. "Go to No. 10, Harringford Square," she said.

The cabman, who knew his fare well enough by sight, and was consequently observant of her looks and tones, wondered at the peremptoriness of the order; and when, twenty minutes later, he drew up at No. 10, Harringford Square, he wondered again at the face he caught sight of as Selma paid him. Her colour fluctuated with every breath she drew, and her hands were shaking so that she could hardly shut her purse. The man drove slowly away, looking back at her as she stood waiting on the doorstep.

"Is Mrs. Roger Cornish at home?" she asked of the woman who opened the door.

"Mrs. Cornish is at home, miss!" was the answer; "but——"

"I know," interrupted Selma. "She is not seeing any one. But I think she will see me. Tell her that Miss Malet is here, please." And with the unconscious arrogance which admiration had bred in her, Selma gave the woman no choice but to obey her.

"This way, miss, please," said the latter meekly, and a moment later Selma found herself alone, where she had been only once before—in Mervyn's drawing-room. She gave one quick glance round and caught her breath sharply, and then she moved to the window and stood there looking out with her hands clasped tightly together, until the sound of the door opening made her turn, as a little fragile figure in deep black ran straight into her arms.

"Oh, Selma!" it cried. "Oh, Selma!" Selma held it to her in a clasp which was almost painful, and there was a silence.

Mervyn was the first to speak. She lifted her face from Selma's shoulder and said in a low, thin little voice, from which all the tone seemed to be gone:

"How good of you to come!"

There were no tears in her eyes; but there was that look on her face which is more pitiful than tears—the look which comes when the first shock is past, when grief is such a close companion that such expression of it is occasional and rare.

"I couldn't keep away," said Selma, impulsively. "Mervyn, I can think of nothing else. Ah, my poor little Mervyn!" she added, with her beautiful eyes full of tears, as she looked into Mervyn's face, so thin and white against her deep mourning.

"Thank you, dear," murmured Mervyn, clinging to her again for a moment. Then she moved and said, "Sit down, dear."

Wifehood, motherhood, or sorrow—perhaps all three combined — had given Mervyn a dignity which sat quite naturally on her now. Except for her first gesture as she ran into Selma's arms, the little demonstrative Mervyn of old days was gone. It was Selma who knelt by her side as she sat down, and took both her hands in hers.

"He suffered so, poor little one," the little, toneless voice went on, as if in answer to the sympathy in the beautiful face lifted to hers. "I remember that always, Selma, and it comforts me." Her voice trembled, and large, heavily-dropping tears rose in her eyes. "One couldn't wish that he should suffer; but Selma, I miss my baby so!"

She turned her head away and leant it against the back of her chair, crying, not passionately, but with the quiet tears which

are all the sadder, because there is no merciful
exhaustion to be hoped from them; and Selma
let her face fall upon the small, cold hands
she held, kissing them softly again and again,
with broken words of sympathy and affection
as Mervyn told her the sad little story of her
baby's life. Her tears had stopped before she
finished, and her voice was only a little weaker
and sadder than it had been from the first, as
though nothing could add to the grief which
nothing but time could lessen. There was a
pause after she finished, and then she looked at
Selma with a faint smile. "I thought I was never
going to see you again, Selma dear," she said.

"It is very good of you to think of me at
all," said Selma. She rose as she spoke, and
took a chair near Mervyn.

"I haven't even seen you act for a long
time," went on Mervyn, with another little ghost
of a smile. "But, of course, I know you are
getting on splendidly. Are you satisfied and
happy, dear?"

Selma laughed lightly. "I've not arrived at the satisfied stage," she said. "That is in the future. But I am on the way to it, I suppose. Every one is very kind to me."

"I'm so glad," returned Mervyn. "I always knew it would be like that. I only wish you weren't always so busy, dear; it's so sad never to see you. I am so sorry Roger should miss you, Selma. He will be so disappointed. He goes to see you act often, and tells me all about it."

"How is he?"

"He is so good and so strong," Mervyn answered, softly, with a loving light in her eyes which made her strangely like and unlike the Mervyn of old days. "He feels it so dreadfully, and he doesn't think of anything but making it easier for me. If you could stay with me a little," she went on, pleadingly, "you would see him. I expect him in early." She waited for an answer; but there was a moment's dead silence. Then Selma rose hurriedly.

"I mustn't stay, I'm afraid," she said. "I only came for a few minutes, because I was so sorry. You'll tell him, Mervyn?"

"He will be so sorry," answered Roger's wife, looking at Selma with a smile which seemed to bring the past very close to them—the past as a peaceful memory, untouched by any trace of bitterness or pain. "He always thinks there is no one like you, and you know I think so too. Good-bye, dear," she added, as Selma bent to kiss her. "I wish you need not go. Oh, Selma, how beautiful you are!"

"Selma, how beautiful you are!" John Tyrrell would have given a good deal, blasé and cynical as he was, to have been able to say the same words when he received Selma in his own house half an hour later. The accusation most frequently brought against Miss Malet's beauty by her detractors was that she wanted colour; she was too pale, they said, and her eyes were too dark. But no such fault could have been found with her now, as she stood in the hall as

Tyrrell explained to her his sister's absence. Her cheeks were flushed and burning with a lovely vivid colour; her eyes looked feverishly large and shining, and glittered and sparkled brilliantly.

"Sybilla will be in directly, no doubt," said Tyrrell, thinking, as he spoke, that he had never seen anything more perfect than her face. "Will you come and let me entertain you in the study until she comes, or would you prefer the state and ceremony of the drawing-room? I am very glad to see you here, Selma," he finished, suddenly dropping the mock deference which was a standing joke between them, and speaking in a tone of quiet cordiality, while his eyes met hers with an expression which they very seldom wore. But Selma's eyes had wandered restlessly away, and she answered:

"It's very kind of you, Mr. Tyrrell. Don't trouble about me, please. One gets rather tired of being entertained, you know."

Her voice was rather hard and sharp, and

there was a certain reckless disregard of the courtesy or discourtesy of her words, not uncommon in spoilt beauties, but new in Selma. Tyrrell looked at her with a slight considering frown. He was not surprised, and he was not particularly disturbed.

"I won't entertain you, then," he said. "Come into the study and we will sit and say nothing!"

"What an inviting prospect!" exclaimed Selma, with a little disdainful laugh which rang sharp as her voice did. "Thank you, Mr. Tyrrell, but I think solitude will suit me better. I will sit and say nothing in my own room, with your kind permission," and, with another mocking laugh, she turned away from him and went quickly upstairs.

Tyrrell returned to his study with a slight smile, and solaced himself with a cigarette. It was a new departure on Selma's part, he told himself, but not on the whole an important one. Half an hour had passed, he had taken up a book, when there was a soft knock at the door, and, before he could speak, Selma came in, straight across the room to where he stood as he rose to receive her.

"I am so sorry," she said, simply, in a low voice. "You are so good to me, and I was so rude. There is nobody so good to me as you are, and I cannot bear to think of your being angry." All the colour was gone from her face, her eyes as she raised them for a moment only to his were dark and heavy, and her pleading voice shook a little.

"Of what are they made?" was Tyrrell's reflection on women in general, as he listened to her and looked at her. "This is another creature!"

"I could never be angry with you, Selma," he said, and even on the stage his voice had never been more beautiful. "Don't you know that nothing you could say to me would make any difference?"

"I know that you are the kindest friend I

have in the world," she said, softly, stretching out her hand as she spoke and letting it rest in his. "It was horrible of me, Mr. Tyrrell. May I sit here with you, now?"

His only answer was a smile as he wheeled her round a chair, and as she sat down, he said:

"Are we to sit and say nothing?"

Selma lifted her eyes to him deprecatingly, and, to his amazement, they were full of tears.

"Let us try and think that it is a long time ago," she said, "a long, long time ago, before I began to come out. Mr. Tyrrell, sometimes I behave as though—as though I had forgotten; but, indeed, in my heart I never do. I know, always, that I owe everything to you—to your help, to your advice. Talk to me as you used to talk when I came here every day, when there was no rush and nobody but you."

"That is a very long time ago, Selma," he returned.

He did not sit down, but stood looking at her beautiful, softened face, with eyes which might have startled her if she had looked up. She did not look up, nor did she make any answer, except a little sad gesture of acquiescence; and, as he watched her, his face paled slightly, and he drew a step nearer to her.

"Selma," he began. But he was interrupted. Before Selma had time to read the expression on his face, the door behind them opened, and Miss Tyrrell's voice said suavely:

"How shocking of me to be so late!"

CHAPTER VI.

A FEW hours after Miss Tyrrell's appearance in her brother's study, there was nothing of which John Tyrrell was more convinced than that he owed her a debt of gratitude for her most timely arrival. A few minutes later, he told himself, and he would have thrown away the self-restraint of two years, he would have deprived himself of all he had diplomatised during the last two months to effect, he would have allowed himself to be deceived by what he knew to be in reality one of the great obstacles in his way, Selma's feelings for him as an old friend; he would have been carried away by the opportunity, by her beauty and gentleness, like a mere boy. The knowledge

gave a shock to his self-respect, to his reliance
on his own judgement, which caused him to
pull himself up sharply, and mature his plans
with a deliberate coolness and self-repression,
intensified by the touch of self-contempt with
which he did it. The air was already full of
reports about himself and Selma, and some of
these reports, it seemed to him, must inevitably
come to her ears before long; but he renewed
his determination to give her time to get
thoroughly used to them. Possibly, he thought,
by the end of the season she might even have
come to the point of wondering why he did
not propose, if every one was expecting him
to do so; in any case, when she should have
arrived at the point of looking upon his doing so
as a matter of probability, her present affectionate
gratitude to him would become a help and not
a hindrance. He would wait until the end of
the season, he resolved, and then he would speak.

The rush of the season grew fast and furious
as May gave place to June, the long days and

short nights—an arrangement of nature transposed by society—went by in an incessant round of gaiety, and among all the fluctuating objects of society's interest, there were two subjects of gossip which never flagged. One was Miss Tyrrell's marriage with Lord Ellingham, which was to take place in the first week of July; the other, infinitely more interesting, as leaving room for unlimited conjecture, was the expected engagement of Miss Malet and Mr. Tyrrell. In one respect only, so far, were Tyrrell's calculations at fault. There was perhaps only one person in the London world who was utterly innocent and ignorant as to any such report, and that person was Selma herself.

Selma was not standing either the fatigues or the admiration of the present season so well as she had stood them during the two last. She was rather harder and more reckless in manner, and she was thinner; but it was said that she was more beautiful than ever for the little flush which was now so often in her cheeks.

The first week of July came with sunshine
such as is not often seen in London, bringing
not only Miss Tyrrell's wedding-day, but also
an event which Helen considered infinitely more
important than any number of fashionable
marriages. Humphrey's picture of "Imogen"
had more than justified the prophecies as to its
being the picture of the year; it had made such
a sensation as no picture, not relying for its
success on the popularity or cheap sentiment
of its subject, had achieved for many years. It
was well understood in the art world that it was
not the temporary sensation of a season, a
popular craze which would die away, to be
succeeded by something different, but the lasting
mark made by a true artist on his time, and
when, in the spring, a vacancy occurred among
the Royal Academicians, it was a foregone con-
clusion among the Associates that Humphrey
Cornish was the man to fill it.

The election took place rather later in the
summer than usual—on the first of July—and

on the following morning Selma, coming downstairs about eleven o'clock, opened the studio
door, and found Humphrey there alone.

"May I come in, Humphrey?" she said,
with a pretty touch in her voice that was half
patronage, half deference. "I want to congratulate the new R.A."

Humphrey turned to her, brush in hand, with
a smile of invitation.

"Come in by all means, Selma," he answered. "I don't see you here often, now."

"No," she assented, with a little sigh as
of a victim to circumstances, as she came up to
look at the work he was doing. "I'm so busy,
Humphrey."

He studied her face for a moment without
speaking. She was looking better that morning
than she had been doing lately—less feverish
and over-excited—but perhaps for that very
reason the rather hard and imperious expression,
which now underlay with always increasing
distinctness all the transient phases which passed

across her face, was more than usually apparent in spite of her smile.

"As you say," said Humphrey, quietly, " you are very busy !"

"It's a regular treadmill," she said, with a light laugh. " I shall retire for the season after Miss Tyrrell's wedding to-morrow, I think. There is not much more to come, and I think I've done my duty. Thank goodness I shall have no more work at the theatre after to-morrow night." The next night was to be the last of Tyrrell's season. "But this is not saying what I came to say," she went on again, with that little touch of patronage which a vainer man than Humphrey could not have resented, it was so pretty and unconscious. "You are really elected, Humphrey! I am so delighted."

"Thanks," answered Humphrey, simply.

"I met your president the other night," she said, "and I told him that if he resigned his own position to you it would be an entirely insufficient reward for the trouble I gave you over the sittings for 'Imogen.' I hope you will bury my shortcomings in oblivion, under the circumstances. This is nice, Humphrey," she added, turning to the canvas by which they were still standing. "What are you going to do with it?"

Almost for the first time Humphrey tacitly declined to discuss his work with her.

"It's only a beginning," he said, lifting it from the easel as he spoke, "I shall not work at it any more this morning."

"It looks pretty," responded Selma, turning carelessly and uncomprehendingly away. "Where is Helen, Humphrey? I want to talk to her before I go out."

All the world was going that afternoon to a large garden party—one of the regular events of the season, and touchingly alluded to by Miss Tyrrell on this occasion as her last appearance. The interest attached to the relation between Selma and Tyrrell in the

eyes of society had heightened as time added
a touch of mystery to them, and every large
party was spiced by the excitement of watching
their proceedings. This particular garden party,
the garden being very large and rambling, had
a reputation for advancing such affairs considerably, and public hope and anticipation
had been concentrated upon it accordingly for
some time past.

"Everybody will be here, of course," sighed
Miss Tyrrell, plaintively, as she and Selma,
followed by Tyrrell, made their way across the
hall through the increasing stream of new
arrivals to the drawing-room, where their hostess
was receiving. "How do you do?" nodding
effusively to some friends who were too far
off to hear her. "It will be dreadfully trying,
dear girl; almost worse than to-morrow," she
added, alluding to her wedding-day with an
agitated flutter which did duty for a blush,
and, before Selma could do more than smile
sympathetically, the human stream behind them

had to stay its course while they were being
shaken hands with by their hostess with the
effusive cordiality due to one of the features
of her party. A few minutes later, Miss
Tyrrell having coyly allowed herself to be ap-
propriated for the moment by Lord Ellingham,
who was one of the first people they met,
Selma and Tyrrell passed slowly through the
animated, smartly-dressed crowd out on to
the terrace together, shaking hands, or bowing
and smiling to every second person they
met.

It was not wonderful that Miss Malet never
entered a room full of people without making
a sensation. There was something about her,
apart from her beauty and grace, apart from
the exquisite self-possession of manner which
social success had brought her, that separated
her from the crowd under any circumstances.
To-day, in one of the soft white frocks which
she affected a great deal that summer, with a
large hat framing her bright and animated face

in curves which seemed to emphasize its beauty, her loveliness was perfect.

There was no pause in the babel of talk and laughter which came from every part of the wide stone terrace ; but there was hardly one among all the crowd of people thronging it from end to end who did not glance at her again and again as she stood with Tyrrell close to her just outside one of the drawing-room windows, talking and laughing with the numerous admirers who had gathered round her directly she appeared.

" By Jove, she is a beauty ! "

The comment was made in a low voice by a man at the extreme end of the terrace, and his companion answered him in the same tone with a laugh, which, slight as it was, was as insolent as the eyes with which he was staring full at Selma.

" Tyrrell is not the man to give himself away as he's doing for nothing," he said. " How long do you give them ? "

It was an unusually wide stone terrace running the whole length of the fine old house, and a flight of three or four wide stone steps with low stone balusters led down to the garden, which stretched away from it; but, large as the terrace was, it provided scarcely breathing space, much less elbow room, for the crowd of people who were congregated on it and on the steps, and there abruptly terminated. Everything was bathed now in glorious July sunshine, the grey stone of the house, which made such an effective background; the gay colours of the women's dresses; the bright flowers and green trees in the garden. But the latter were brilliant and sparkling with moisture. A great deal of rain had fallen in the night, and even in the morning, and only a few enterprising spirits had ventured forth from the terrace to walk up and down on the wet grass and gravel; consequently, the guests invited with a view to the space afforded by the lawns and walks, were politely squeezing one another to the verge of suffocation in a space which would not comfortably have accommodated a quarter of the number.

It was evidently the thing to remain on the terrace; but Selma had not reigned for two seasons for nothing, and she objected strongly and speedily.

"It's suffocating!" she was saying to Tyrrell, as she stood at the top of the steps. "How stupid to stay here! Let us go and see who is in the garden. No; I don't want to speak to Lady Latter, Mr. Tyrrell," she added, imperiously, as he returned the bow of that lady, who was making her way slowly in their direction. "I don't like her, and I don't know how you can. Come along!"

Lady Latter had several men in attendance, and she was talking and laughing as recklessly as usual; but her eyes were following Tyrrell and Selma as they passed alone together a few paces down the garden, before Miss Malet became again the centre of a small group of

people who had come up from the lawn to shake
hands.

One of Lady Latter's train saw the direction
in which she was looking, and laughed.

"Tyrrell's in luck," he said—he was rather
young and inexperienced, and Lady Latter was
educating him, she said. "When will it be
announced, I wonder?" And then he caught
Lady Latter's eye, and wondered what in the
world he had said to make her look as she did.

"Possibly," she said, with an odd ring in
her voice, "when there is something to be
announced! Don't be so knowing, Jack!"

"I'm not!" he protested, eagerly, and in-
advertently. "I mean," as she laughed, "it's a
fact, you know. Every one says so. I can't
think why they should go on keeping it dark,
when everybody knows it."

"It does seem odd," returned Lady Latter,
derisively. "Jack, don't be a fool!"

There was no derision in her eyes, though,
and she seemed to be hardly aware when her

disciple excused himself rather huffily, and departed. Her face was hard and preoccupied, and it had not softened or altered at all, though she had exchanged many words and much rather loud laughter on her way, when a few minutes later she found her way to where Miss Tyrrell was holding a farewell reception.

"Dear Lady Latter," Miss Tyrrell exclaimed, pressing the hand Lady Latter offered her, tenderly—there was hardly a woman in London for whom she had a greater natural dislike. "I was afraid I should miss you. It is so difficult to see every one."

"It is difficult to see any one in such a crush," returned Lady Latter. She paused an instant, and then went on, with a laugh which grated painfully on Miss Tyrrell's refined and artistic ear: "And I think we are all occupied in watching the progress of your brother's little romance. It's really too kind of him to give us so much to talk about."

Miss Tyrrell replied with a little non-

M 2

committal laugh she had adopted for such occasions, and Lady Latter drew a little closer to her.

"It must be a great relief to you to feel that you are not leaving your brother alone for long," she said, and the words contrasted oddly with the hard tone in which she spoke, and with the expression of her eyes, as they rested on Miss Tyrrell's face. Miss Tyrrell saw only the opportunity for an attitude and not the trap, and fell into the latter with promptitude and despatch. "It is!" she said. "It is! How could I have brought myself to leave him alone?"

"Then he is going to marry her?" Lady Latter's tone was carelessness itself; but there was a note in it which brought Miss Tyrrell to herself with a sudden cold shock of reality, though she could not have said the next instant what had so startled her. She had said rather more than she had meant to say, but it was of no consequence, she thought.

"Now that is hardly fair, dear Lady Latter," she said, "to take advantage of me like that! But, as it is you who ask the question, I don't mind admitting the truth. As it is not public property yet, however, I need not ask you to say nothing, I am sure."

Lady Latter laughed again.

"To say nothing!" she said, in what Miss Tyrrell condemned as a singularly inartistic voice. "No! I shall say nothing, of course! What has become of Miss Malet? Oh, there she is on the lawn!"

Lady Latter stood for a moment, motionless, with her black eyes fixed upon Selma with an expression which struck Miss Tyrrell as peculiarly unpleasant. Then she moved away without another word.

"She is certainly the rudest woman in London!" was Miss Tyrrell's mental comment.

Selma's movement towards the garden had been followed by half the people on the terrace, and she and Tyrrell had drifted apart in the moving kaleidoscope of men and women into which the smooth lawn was transformed. She was standing at the end of the garden, talking to Julian Heriot, and as the stream continued to flow from the terrace she laughed lightly.

" I came off the terrace to get away from the crowd," she said, " and now the crowd is here! How delicious this garden would be with no one in it."

" Am I to take that as a hint, Miss Malet ? " was Heriot's response.

" No, no ! " she answered, laughing, " of course not ! Only a garden always seems to me to be spoilt by this kind of thing, don't you know. It should be quiet and peaceful." There was a look in her eyes, as she spoke, which Heriot had very seldom seen in them—a look as though the picture her words had brought before her had touched her. She turned away from the crowd as she finished, and Heriot walked by her side, looking at her for a moment, before he said, rather suddenly :

" Tyrrell will miss his sister very much."

Selma started as though his words had recalled her to the present, and lifted a pair of innocent, unconscious eyes to his face.

" I'm afraid he will," she said. " Poor Mr. Tyrrell! It is rather sad for him, isn't it?"

" He will marry, perhaps," said Heriot, his dark, cynical eyes looking straight into hers. Selma came to a full stop, her cheeks flushing with astonishment and amusement.

" Marry!" she cried. " Mr. Tyrrell marry! Oh, what an idea, Mr. Heriot!"

" Is there any reason against it?" returned Heriot, carelessly moving to continue their walk. " He is quite eligible."

" I suppose he is," said Selma, thoughtfully. " I wonder why he never has married. How odd it would be!"

" Should you be pleased, Miss Malet?"

" I?" answered Selma, glancing at him with wondering eyes. " I? Yes—of course, I suppose I should, if he married a nice woman."

Julian Heriot made no comment, and they strolled on in silence for a few minutes. They had wandered gradually—and unconsciously on Selma's part—away from the crush on the lawn down a shady path which led to the second garden, separated from the other by a high old yew hedge. At the bottom of the path, Selma turned absently, as if to retrace their steps, and Heriot stopped short.

"Miss Malet," he said, "I'm going to make a fool of myself." He spoke so quietly that Selma glanced at him in doubt as to whether she had heard aright, and then she saw that his thin, clever face was quite white, even to the lips. "Nobody could be more keenly alive than I am," he pursued, deliberately, "to the imbecility of what I am going to say. I've argued the matter out with myself over and over again. There's not the faintest reason why you should like me; you've given me no more encouragement than you've given to dozens of men. I should be a preposterous match for you. There's nothing to be said against it that I've not said to myself. But, Miss Malet, will you be my wife?"

Selma had heard him through with a face which, by the time he ended, was nearly as white as his own. She had heard the last words, many a time before, from all sorts of men, and had answered them gently always, though often with little distress of mind for the speaker. But, in this case, not only was the shock of surprise inexpressible, but there was something in Julian Heriot's tone and manner—something desperately hopeless and reckless, in spite of his perfect quiet, that made the position terribly painful.

"Oh, Mr. Heriot!" she said, in a low, grieved voice. "Oh, Mr. Heriot!"

"I am not quite idiot enough," he went on, in the same tone, "to think of telling you what I feel. I've not had much respect for love all my life, and I can't talk about it now. Very likely I shouldn't make you happy, I've never made myself happy ; but—I would try." He stopped abruptly, and a little soft cry came from Selma.

"Please don't say any more," she said. "I'm very, very sorry, Mr. Herriot ; but it's impossible, it's quite impossible. Oh, what can I say ?"

A little twitch passed across his face, and there was an instant's silence. Then he said :

"Thanks. Don't trouble. It was my mistake entirely. Shall we go back now ?"

"I am so sorry, Mr. Heriot."

"Please don't think of it," he repeated, turning as he spoke, and moving by her side in the direction from which they had come. "Beautiful grounds these are, aren't they ?" The indomitable cynicism which would not spare its own pain even to the extent of acknowledging it, the contrast between the last words and the set white face with which he spoke, shook Selma as no words could have done. She could do or say nothing to make it easier for him ; but she could spare him the polite conversation he evidently intended to compel himself to keep up; and she sat down on a garden seat which was fitted into a recess cut in the thick yew hedge.

"I will stop here for a little while, I think," she said; "it is so hot. Don't—don't let me keep you, Mr. Heriot." She held out her hand as she spoke, lifting her eyes for an instant to his face. He took her hand, pressed it for a moment sharply in his, and then dropped it and turned away, leaving her without another word.

Selma watched him out of sight with liquid, pitying eyes, and, as he disappeared, the expression seemed to die gradually out of her face, leaving it very still and inexpressibly weary. It was very quiet in that empty corner of the large garden; from the distance came the hum of voices and laughter, and from farther off still —a strange background to the quiet around her —the wonderful subdued roar of London; but the trees were motionless in the hot July sunshine, and the air was almost oppressively still.

Selma had not moved, she was sitting just as
Heriot had left her, a graceful white figure out-
lined by the dark yew hedge behind her, every
line of her pale, tired face relaxed and softened,
and with an absent look in her dark eyes, when
she became vaguely conscious of voices some-
where near her, and roused herself slowly with a
little sigh. She turned her head to listen, and
from the other side of the hedge, her own name,
uttered by a voice she did not know, caught her
ear.

"Selma Malet? No, I've not been introduced."

Selma rose, as she heard the words, with a
little smile, and stooped to pick up her sunshade
which lay on the seat by her side. As she did
so her movement was suddenly arrested, her lips
did not close, though the smile was a smile no
longer, as the next words in the same unknown
voice fell on her ears.

"She's the saddest sight I've seen for many
a day !"

Selma did not catch the answer. She was conscious of a certain confusion of brain for a moment, and then it seemed to clear again as the voice resumed.

"A great success you call her! My dear fellow, she is the most pitiable failure in London. She has genius—splendid genius, and she is crushing it out as fast as may be in the mill of society."

She was standing upright now, white, and trembling a little. There was a confused murmur of response, and then she heard:

"Look at it for yourself! You remember her when she first came out, and you saw her the other night. The actual deterioration in her is appalling. She made a failure last year; if she had made such another this year it might have startled her! A success? A mockery! She has such a genius that it lights up, in spite of herself, a performance below mediocrity! There is no work, no thought, no art in what she does, only the innate power which she has not yet suppressed. I wonder whether she will have to answer some day for what she has wasted!"

She was leaning back against the hedge, her two hands clutching one another painfully, and a little inaudible gasp came from between her white lips. She had no consciousness of listening, no consciousness of anything but the dreadful, passionless, unknown voice, which seemed to have come out of the silence to tell her the truth.

"They said when she first came out that she meant working—that she was an artist at heart. I wonder whether she really supposes that this society business has anything to do with art, or I wonder how she reconciles it with her old ideas. She must have had ideas when she played Bianca! By Jove! only two years ago! And now she's content to be the fashion! It's moral suicide."

A resistless wave of roaring, hissing sound seemed to surge up over Selma's brain, drowning everything else, and when it subsided again

everything was still and quiet as it had been
when she sat alone on the garden seat. The
owner of the voice had passed on.

A quarter of an hour later one of the
men-servants came up to Miss Tyrrell in the
garden.

"Miss Malet told me to tell you that she
was gone home, madam," he said.

CHAPTER VII.

Miss Tyrrell had given it to be understood
from the first that her wedding was to be a
"quiet little affair"; she should allow her
brother to give no party, she declared; but
she hoped that all her friends would come
and say good-bye to her. She had hoped
this on two or three hundred printed cards
of invitation, and on the afternoon after the
garden party, the "quiet little affair" was
lining with carriages the street in which the
Tyrrells lived, crowding the drawing-room to
the verge of suffocation, and filling the
staircase with a confused mass of human
beings, struggling up to the drawing-room
door, where "Lady Ellingham," in a wedding-

dress which was to be a revelation of the beautiful to the conventional herd, was receiving her numerous friends.

Lady Ellingham's smile was sweetness itself; Lady Ellingham's affectionate cordiality to all comers was unvarying; but there was the faintest shadow of annoyance about her nevertheless. To the heroine of an occasion it is distinctly annoying to hear another woman's name incessantly on the lips of the crowd assembled to do honour to herself; to know that another woman is the centre of much talk and conjecture, when public attention should be by rights concentrated on the said heroine. And every one of Lady Ellingham's guests was asking the same question in slightly varied forms. "Where is Miss Malet?" "What an extraordinary thing that Miss Malet is not here!" "Is it true that Miss Malet is not coming?" Selma was not there.

Lady Ellingham had given utterance over

and over again, with the utmost suavity, to the explanation she had decided to offer, of what was to her quite as extraordinary and inexplicable a proceeding as any of her guests found it. And when the question was put to her for about the fiftieth time, she was still smilingly regretful.

"I am sorry to say she is not well enough to be here," she said. "I had a little note from her this morning. Dear girl, I am so grieved."

Lady Ellingham did not think it for the public good that she should mention that the little note she had indeed received from Selma that morning had contained no information whatever as to the writer's health, but had said simply, in the fewest possible words, that she could not come to the wedding. Nor did she think it necessary to publish it abroad that the note in question had so astonished and disconcerted her that she had taken it straight to her brother in his study, and had watched his face curiously as he read it.

Tyrrell had glanced through it, and then sat silent for a moment frowning thoughtfully.

"Better say she is ill," he had said, finally, giving the note back to his sister and returning to his work, and Miss Tyrrell had discreetly retired, burning with mixed curiosity and indignation.

The "little affair" went off brilliantly, in spite of Miss Malet's absence. At about half-past four it was hardly possible to move in the drawing-room, on the stairs, or in the tea-room, and Tyrrell at the foot of the staircase, and desirous of putting in an appearance in his drawing-room above, was wondering how he was to do it, when he became aware of Julian Heriot standing against the wall close to him.

"I'm afraid you're wedged in there," said Tyrrell, pleasantly. "How are you?"

"How are you?" returned the other, answering the conventional greeting with its equally conventional response. "Are you pro-

posing to go up those stairs?" glancing up at
them with a slight smile as he spoke.

"Well, on the whole, I think not; not this
minute at least!" returned Tyrrell, laughing.
"Have you been in this corner ever since you
arrived, Heriot?"

It was a kind of tiny recess in the hall,
into which Heriot had stepped back out of
the crowd, and as Tyrrell stood in front of
him, letting the clatter of many tongues round
them dominate his voice, they were inaudible
to every one but each other, and were practically alone in the midst of the crush about
them. Heriot did not answer Tyrrell's question.
There was a moment's pause between them,
and then he said, looking straight before him
at the crowded staircase with no alteration of
his usual expression:

"Miss Malet is not here to-day, they say!"

"No!" answered Tyrrell. "She has knocked
herself up, I'm sorry to say."

"I made a fool of myself yesterday,"

pursued Heriot, in the same unmoved voice, drowned for all but Tyrrell by the noise of other voices. "I proposed to Miss Malet, and she refused me, of course." He paused an instant, as though something in the crowd had caught his eye. Tyrrell, completely taken by surprise, waited in silence, eyeing him with eyes which had suddenly grown very hard and cold. "I don't argue from that very natural circumstance that there must inevitably be some one else," Heriot went on; "unless I misunderstood her altogether, she is not engaged." He had spoken the last words very slowly and deliberately, and he paused and looked Tyrrell straight in the face as he finished. "Don't you think it is time she was?" he said, quietly.

The two men faced one another for a moment, and Tyrrell tried in vain to read the cynical, impassive face before him. Then he said, carelessly, taking the other's words intentionally in the simple sense in which he knew they were not meant:

"Perhaps! But she is younger than she looks, you know. Well, I suppose I must try to get upstairs. See you again!"

He turned away, dismissing Heriot and his words from his mind, until it should be convenient to him to reflect upon them.

He did not understand them, but the present was by no means the time for explanations. He had his duties, as host, to attend to, and he attended to them accordingly with the delightful manner which was one of his greatest social charms. Julian Heriot watched him for a little while moving to and fro in the crowd—he himself best knowing how—and then he went away.

That same afternoon Humphrey Cornish, oppressed with a sense that the day was coming when he must take his holiday, which he hated prospectively, and during which he revelled undemonstratively in country sights and sounds, had settled down to follow up a hard morning's work with two or three

hours more of the same kind. He had been
alone in the quiet studio for more than an
hour, working with concentrated, thoughtful
face, so absorbed that he did not even look
round when the door opened and shut again
softly. He was vaguely conscious that Helen
had come in and was sitting now with her
needlework in her accustomed place at the
other end of the room as he had been
vaguely conscious before of missing her
presence. And he had no idea that half an
hour had passed since her entrance, when
he said, absently, without pausing in his
work :

"How is she?"

Helen held her needle suspended in her
hand as she lifted her head to answer. She
was quite accustomed to Humphrey's ways,
and accepted them simply as part of the
man she loved when she could not understand
them.

"She says her head is better. She didn't

open the door, and I hope she was lying down," she answered, softly. "The sun must have been too hot for her yesterday," she added, meditatively, and then there was silence again in the studio as Humphrey continued his work, and Helen bent her head over the little soft white frock she was making for the little Helen. Another half-hour passed, and then the silence was broken a second time. There was a man's quick step on the stair, a step which caused Helen to lay down her work with a low exclamation of surprise, as Roger Cornish came into the room.

"Why, Roger!" said Helen, holding out her hand to him, while Humphrey was reconciling himself to the conviction that he was interrupted, "what a surprising time of day to see you!"

Roger was rather flushed, and he shook hands with Helen absently and awkwardly, making no apology, as he usually did, for in-

terrupting his brother's work when Humphrey
collected his ideas with an effort and received
him with a cordial "Hullo, Roger!" He
seemed hardly to hear Helen's words; he replied to her question as to Mervyn's health
vaguely and as though his thoughts were preoccupied, and after a few minutes he said,
abruptly :

"Helen, don't think me the roughest fellow
you know if I ask Humphrey to come downstairs with me. I've got some business to talk
to him about."

Helen rose, laughing at him pleasantly as she
did so.

"Of course, Roger!" she answered. "But
you shan't go downstairs. I'm going to see
whether Selma is asleep." She left the room
as she spoke, and Roger turned sharply to his
brother.

"Is she ill?" he said, in a low, quick
tone.

"Selma?" answered Humphrey, looking at

him. "No; only over-tired. What's wrong, Roger? Sit down."

"I can't sit down," returned Roger, vehemently, turning and beginning to pace restlessly up and down the room. "I've come to you, because I've turned over everything, and I can't think of any other way. You're her brother, or the next thing to it, and the only man, I suppose, who has a right to interfere. Humphrey, do you know that she's — talked about?"

The last words came from him hurried and almost muffled, and there was that about them which no man could misunderstand. Humphrey moved suddenly, with a short, sharp exclamation, and then there was a moment's dead silence. It was broken by Humphrey.

"Are you speaking of Selma?" he said.

Roger had come to a sudden stop as he spoke his last words, and was standing facing his brother, his breath coming very quick and short, his face flushed darkly.

"Yes!" he said, hoarsely. "You know how I felt for her once, Humphrey. You know that she's nothing to me now but an ideal; but, by Heaven, I'd give all I've got—except my wife—for your right to bring that fellow to book!"

The first moment of fierce indignation over, his brother's passion had the effect of bringing Humphrey to a quieter estimate of the case. Dreamer and recluse as he was by temperament, he had far more knowledge of the London world than Roger; and the idea, though it was no less intolerable, was less inconceivable to him than to his brother.

"Who is it?" he said, shortly and sternly.

Roger broke into a fierce, harsh laugh.

"The man she looked upon as a kind of guardian," he said. "The man, of all others, who ought to have kept every breath of scandal from her name. Scandal, good Heavens, and Selma! John Tyrrell!"

Then he told his brother, in short, sharp

sentences, of the words he had heard the night before at his club—the words which had been cut short, and turned into a sullen apology, by such a fierce outburst from himself as had reduced the whole roomful to silence.

"Perhaps I made the thing worse by making such a row," he finished, ruefully. "Every one heard, and they'll talk more, confound them! If she should hear, Humphrey! Good Heavens, if she should hear!"

There was no answer, and he turned and began to pace fiercely up and down the room again. Humphrey was sitting with a clenched hand resting on the arm of his chair, and a set, roused expression on his face. He was thinking of the headache which Helen had found so perplexing in her sister that day; and he was thinking that if such shameful gossip had come to Selma's ears, a horsewhip would be a mild instrument with which to approach the man who had been so careless as to render such a catastrophe even remotely possible.

"What's to be done?" demanded Roger, abruptly, pulling up suddenly and facing his brother. Humphrey rose, and his voice, as he spoke, was very stern and resonant.

"I shall see Tyrrell to-night," he said; and Roger, who had wished from the bottom of his heart that it was he and not the impractical Humphrey who stood to Selma in the place of a brother, was reassured by the expression of his brother's face.

Helen was somewhat surprised when she came back to the studio an hour later, thinking that any amount of business might have been discussed in that time, to find Humphrey alone, walking slowly up and down the room with a grave, preoccupied face. She was a little surprised again later in the evening when he told her after dinner that he was going out.

He had determined to go to Tyrrell at the theatre—the only place where he could be sure of finding him—and he sent in a note, asking courteously, but in words which hardly admitted

of a refusal, for a few minutes after the performance, and requesting Tyrrell to say nothing to
his sister-in-law on the subject. He received in
return an equally courteous reply, and accordingly, at a little before eleven o'clock, he was
shown into the room where Tyrrell transacted
his business, and left there with the information,
"Mr. Tyrrell will be off in a minute, if you'll
sit down, sir ! "

Humphrey did not sit down, however. He
stood on the hearthrug with that instinct that
leads a man to take up a position near the fireplace, whether the season is summer or winter,
and contemplated the room with stern, unseeing
eyes. It was a comfortable-looking room, with
a curious, indefinable similarity of character to
Tyrrell's study in his own house, though it was
very simply furnished. Everything in it was in
the same perfect taste. The pictures, all connected
in one way or another with Tyrrell's profession,
were old and valuable engravings, the writing-
table here was only larger than the table which

gave the other room its character. But even
the engravings did not attract Humphrey's
attention, and he was standing very much in
the position he had originally taken up, when,
a few minutes later, Tyrrell came into the room.

"I hope you've not been waiting," he said,
courteously. "We are a few minutes later than
usual to-night. Won't you sit down ?" Tyrrell
was looking remarkably handsome ; he was still
wearing his stage dress, a dark, picturesque
costume, which suited him admirably, and made
him look ten years younger than he really was.
He waited while Humphrey, with a quiet
"Thanks !" took the chair he indicated, and
then seated himself, saying with a smile, as he
did so :

"I am sorry to say I have had no opportunity
of transgressing your injunction as to not letting
Miss Malet know of your being here, even if I
had wished it. She has over-tired herself, I am
afraid. I have hardly spoken to her to-night
until a few minutes ago. She has been looking

so ill all the evening. I hope I shall find her better to-morrow."

"You are coming to see her to-morrow?" said Humphrey.

"She has just asked me to come up to your house to-morrow afternoon," returned Tyrrell, with another smile.

There was a moment's silence. Humphrey was thinking that if Selma had heard of the gossip about, she would hardly have asked Tyrrell to come and see her, and it made his present business simpler in his eyes that it should be between himself and Tyrrell, two men, alone. Tyrrell, considering that quite enough had been said in the way of polite preliminary, was waiting for Humphrey to come to the point of the interview, and his face was quietly attentive and business-like when Humphrey began, sternly:

"It is as Miss Malet's brother that I am here to-night, and my business is not pleasant. I have to ask you, Mr. Tyrrell, whether you are aware of the reports abroad?"

Tyrrell's face changed slightly. He was surprised, but not, on the whole, displeased.

"Reports?" he said, easily. "London is
a splendid hot-bed for reports. May I ask
you to explain?"

Humphrey looked at him for a moment
without speaking. With the words he had
heard from Roger in his ears there was something about the careless attitude and manner
of the other as he sat, leaning slightly forward,
that stirred his indignation to white heat.

"I will explain," he said, his voice ringing
with the same strong feeling with which his
usually quiet eyes were alight and glowing.
And in a few short unsparing sentences he
told Tyrrell what Roger had told him.

The words had hardly passed his lips
before Tyrrell rose abruptly with a low, fierce
exclamation.

"Good Heavens!" he said. "Good Heavens,
Cornish!"

Humphrey made no response. The spoken

words and their effect upon Tyrrell had brought the situation into vivid relief in his mind, and his force was concentrated in rigid self-control. He sat quite motionless with his clenched hand resting heavily on the table, his face set and his lips compressed. Tyrrell stood with one arm resting on the mantelpiece, half turned away from him, and there was a moment of dead silence.

With all his foresight and knowledge of the world, such a contingency as that with which he was now brought face to face had never occurred to John Tyrrell. Unconsciously to himself, the relationship as master and pupil, which had existed so long between himself and Selma ; the semi-guardianship which he had exercised over her; perhaps even to some extent the perfect innocence in Selma herself, which rendered the idea of "talk" in connection with her name absolutely inconceivable, had coloured all his theories and all his schemes. His first instinct as he realised the whole significance of the position, was the natural manly one of burning resentment and indignation, so deep as to hold him absolutely speechless. Julian Heriot's words of that very afternoon flashed into his mind; they were only too comprehensible to him now, and the thought that he and many others had heard the words which Humphrey Cornish had just repeated to him made him clench his teeth fiercely.

Humphrey was the first to master himself The tide of anger retreated and left him stern and dignified to the consideration of the present pressing necessity.

"I won't insult my sister," he said, "by saying that I am not here to ask for any explanation from you. We have all been more or less to blame. We should have remembered the possibility of the world's forgetting—what we, of course, never forget—that Selma has no older friend than you." Humphrey paused a moment as he realised afresh how unpardonable it was that it should indeed be Selma's oldest friend who had been so careless of her. "The mistake has been made," he resumed; "the present point is to retrieve it as far as may be. The contradiction of the reports lies with you, of course. It must be done effectually and quietly, and it must be done at once. How do you propose to set about it?"

Tyrrell lifted his head slowly, and turned. During the short interval that had elapsed since his first exclamation, his anger had been succeeded by a swift realisation of all the advantages and disadvantages involved in this new turn of events. In his indomitable determination to possess, sooner or later, that for which he had waited so long and with such relentless self-restraint, there was no instrument which fate could have placed in his hand which he would long have hesitated to use. Things had gone much further than he had intended; his foresight had been less perfect than he imagined; and whether the present circumstances were or were not in his favour was a question he could not decide. But, at least, they brought the crisis. He had heard every word Humphrey had spoken ; but his brain had been at work without a second's intermission, and when the moment arrived for him to speak he was prepared.

"Mr. Cornish," he said, slowly, " I am going to tell you what I know will surprise you. This comes more heavily on me than you have any idea of, because I love your sister. I should have asked her long ago to be my wife if I had thought I had a chance with her."

No course of action on Tyrrell's part, no words he could have spoken could have been more electrifying to Humphrey Cornish. Too completely taken by surprise for the moment to find words, he rose to his feet, and as he stood confronting the handsome, resolute face before him, Tyrrell continued, and his manner was very dignified and very good :

" I need not tell you how inexpressibly I regret it if any carelessness of mine has given rise to these reports. I need not tell you that I was in complete ignorance of them. Under the circumstances, of course, I shall delay no longer. I shall take my chance with your sister when I see her to-morrow. If she accepts me——" he stopped and then finished quietly, " whether she accepts me or not, you may rely on there being no more reports ! "

They looked one another in the face for a moment more, and then with a sense that the ground was cut away from under his feet, that nothing could ever surprise him again, and that there was nothing left for him to do or say, Humphrey held out his hand.

" Thank you," he said, simply ; " I should have relied on you in any case. Under the circumstances there is nothing for me to say, except that I shall hope to congratulate you to-morrow. Good night ! "

" Good night ! " returned Tyrrell, courteously, " and thank you for your good wishes ! To-morrow afternoon ! "

CHAPTER VIII.

THE light was perfect, and his picture was in an extremely interesting stage; but at three o'clock the next afternoon, Humphrey Cornish gave up the attempt at work, which had been more or less unsuccessful all the day, and determined to go out for a walk. His thoughts were running on Selma, unconnectedly but incessantly, and they all turned eventually to one end—his disappointment in her.

He had been thinking of her as she had been when she was looking forward to that first appearance which Roger's coming had prevented—a young girl full of enthusiasm and devotion to her work. Perhaps no one in those days had better appreciated than

Humphrey the genius which was in her, no
one had certainly so sympathised with the
genuine artist spirit which had been hers. He
had watched her and understood her as only
a kindred spirit could have done, and his
sympathy had had in it always a touch of
pity for the pain life was so likely to bring,
when the depths of her nature should be stirred,
to so passionate and sensitive a creature. He
had told himself often in those days that she
would probably suffer, but he had thought of
the suffering that perfects.

He had watched her during the terrible
struggle which had preceded the breaking of
her engagement with Roger; had watched her,
understanding the resistless impulse under which
she struggled, with little doubt as to what the
end must be, and with a sad conviction that
it was better she should reach that end unaided.
He had believed that a collision between her
heart and her artist nature was inevitable, not
knowing of the prompting she had received,

and he had looked to her after life to justify her choice. And now for the past two years he had known that she was deteriorating— deteriorating day by day as artist and as woman, until his old belief in her was utterly destroyed, his hope for her was shattered.

As Tyrrell had believed that she had grasped at society life in wounded pride and disappointment, Humphrey had believed that she was looking for forgetfulness. That she should apparently find it in admiration, in popularity, in the noise and rush of fashionable life, was what he had not expected; it had destroyed his faith in her as nothing else could have done. Would she marry Tyrrell ? he asked himself, sadly. Marry him, perhaps, for his position, perhaps for old friendship's sake. He had little doubt that she would.

He put aside his palette and brushes and went out of the room, and down to the hall, and, as he took his hat, Helen came downstairs to him. She had the little Helen in her arms, a dainty baby figure in its cool white sunbonnet, with the fair little face all smiles, and dimples, and brown eyes, and she was laughing and talking to her as she came.

"Are you going out, dear?" she said, happily. "Baby is going out too; I'm waiting for nurse to take her. We thought it was very hot in the nursery, didn't we, my precious?" pressing her cheek against the soft baby face, which was so like it. "No, sweetheart, father doesn't want you now," she added, hugging the little thing with a delighted laugh, as the little plump arms made demonstrations towards Humphrey. "Shall you be long, dear?"

"Not very, Nell!" he answered, smiling at her and at the laughing face under the white sun-bonnet.

"It's a lovely day," she responded. "I wish Selma could go out. Humphrey, I'm not satisfied about her, dear; she looks so dreadfully ill."

"She has been going out too much," said

Humphrey, as he opened the door. "Good-bye, Nell." He kissed both the Helens—the little one as well as the big one—and went out.

Helen stood on the threshold in the sunshine smiling after him as he went, and as she went back into the hall with the baby in her arms, laughing and conversing after her present undeveloped fashion, she started and smiled; Selma was standing at the foot of the stairs.

"How quietly you came down, dear!" she exclaimed. "Are you rested? You look like a ghost, you are so pale!"

But it was not pallor alone that had so changed the beautiful face. The forty-eight hours which had passed since the garden party had taken every trace of colour from Selma's cheeks—from her very lips—and her eyes were sunken and hollow; but, however they had been passed, those hours had left deeper traces yet. There was a still stricken look in the white face — a look which changed it as no passion of anguish could have done. She did not move as Helen spoke to her, taking no notice of the little Helen's eager, inarticulate calls to her, and she stood in the same position, with one hand resting on the balusters, as she said, in a low, toneless voice:

"I came to tell you that I have business with Mr. Tyrrell when he comes this afternoon. You will not let any one be shown in?"

"Of course not, dear!" returned Helen, cheerily. "Go into the drawing-room, and wait there for him quietly. You shan't be disturbed!" She opened the drawing-room door, close to which she was standing, as she spoke, and looked in. "It is nice and cool," she said. "Let me see you comfortably settled before I go upstairs."

Selma took her hand from the balusters and moved slowly to the door, and on the threshold Helen put her arm round her to draw her on.

"Why, you are quite cold, Selma!" she exclaimed.

"Am I?" said Selma, in the same toneless voice. "I will sit here, in the sun."

She sat down as she spoke, and Helen drew up a blind that the sun might fall more freely upon her.

"There!" she said, "now you can't be cold long. Good-bye, dear!" She bent down as she spoke to kiss her sister, and as she did so the baby in her arms stretched out two little soft hands and stroked the white face with a soft murmur. "Kiss poor auntie, then!" said Helen, merrily. "Selma, how fond she is of you!"

Selma did not answer. For an instant, as the warm, dimpled cheek touched hers, she pressed her face closely against it, and then the two Helens went away together turning two happy, smiling faces towards her from the door, that the little one might blow her a parting kiss.

Selma did not move. She made no change in her attitude, though the chair she had taken was one in which she never sat, and in which she looked curiously rigid and unnatural. She sat there for nearly twenty minutes, looking straight before her, with her dark eyes absolutely expressionless; but the July sun in which she sat did not apparently warm her, for when the door-bell rang at last, she shivered again painfully. She moved for the first time a minute later, when John Tyrrell was shown into the room.

"What a delicious day!" he said, as he came towards her. "I hope you are better for it?" And then he stopped suddenly, shocked and startled for the moment at the sight of her face. "I am sorry to see that you look very ill!" he said, gravely.

He held out his hand as he spoke, and before Selma took it there was a hardly perceptible pause. As he came into the room she had flushed crimson, and the flush had been succeeded by the deadly whiteness which had called forth his last words. The same deep, painful colour

came to her cheeks again as she placed her
hand in his, and to his astonishment, though
she was standing in a flood of afternoon sunshine, her hand as he touched it was cold as
ice.

"I am not ill," she said, quietly. "Thank
you for coming."

Short as it was, Tyrrell had noticed the
interval which had elapsed before she took his
hand, and had noticed her change of colour, and
an idea had flashed across his mind, which was
strengthened as she spoke by something new
and indefinable in her manner to him—something cold and distant, which seemed to make
their old familiar intercourse a thing of the
past. Was it possible, he asked himself, that
she had heard what Humphrey Cornish had
repeated to him last night? The thought was
an eminently disagreeable one; and as Selma
sat down again, and he followed her example,
he took advantage of her silence to review the
position of affairs, and rapidly readjust his

plan of campaign to provide for this unexpected contingency.

The silence was broken by Selma. She had reseated herself in the same constrained, uncharacteristic attitude, as though some painful mental tension affected her whole personality. Her voice as she spoke was thin and hard.

"I asked you to come and see me," she began, "because it seemed to me that I should owe you an explanation."

"An explanation!" repeated Tyrrell. He had put away his thoughts the instant she spoke, and was leaning forward with quiet solicitude, every sense keenly alert and ready to turn anything that might occur to his own ends. "I have told you very often that you never owe me anything," he said with a smile. He was looking straight into her face, and, as she met his eyes, she drew back suddenly and shivered again slightly. She seemed to put something away from her mental consciousness with an effort before she went on :

" I want to say first that I have been thinking only for myself; one can never see for
other people." She paused a moment and then
continued: " But one sees things for oneself
sometimes, and then one must act. I have been
waked up."

She stopped, catching her breath for an
instant. She was looking, not at him, but
straight beyond him; and if, as she said, she
had been waked, her face was as the face of
a woman who has waked face to face with
death. Tyrrell watched her, wondering and
waiting until her words should give him some
clue on which to speak.

"I saw it all at once," she went on, in the
same subdued tone. "And I have thought it
all out since. I have let myself be dazzled
and carried away by excitement, and admiration,
and popularity. I have lost sight of truth and
reality. I have forgotten the end."

She paused again—her eyes very large and
dark—and then on Tyrrell's consciousness there

dawned for the first time a slight glimmer of a bare possibility that there might be something in the girl before him of which he had never, as yet, had any conception. Before he could recover himself sufficiently to speak, Selma had resumed in a quiet, unemotional way.

"I thought it right to tell you," she said, "that I am going to work again. I shall not go out any more. If I have thrown it all away—if it is too late—I can work all my life at least."

"Will you tell me what you mean?" said Tyrrell, quietly.

"Haven't I told you?" she answered, in the same unmoved way, turning her white, still face towards him. "I have seen the truth about the life I have been leading. I know now that it is all false and a mistake; that work and art have nothing to do with it; that nothing true or strong can ever come of it. I did not know—at least, I did not think—

I let myself believe it was all in the day's work. But now I know."

Tyrrell experienced the sensation of a man who has worked his way with infinite care and thought through numberless devious lanes and alleys to find himself, when he thought himself absolutely at his goal, face to face with a blank wall. For all possible contingencies he thought he had prepared, and now he found himself face to face with something he had never dreamed of. She was not thinking of him; she had passed out of the world in which he lived and schemed, into a sphere where none of his plans could help him.

He leant back in his chair, looked at Selma for a moment without speaking; then he said, gently:

"What has suggested all this to you, Selma?" He spoke partly with a desire to gain time, partly with the idea of getting some more extended idea of her state of mind, and neither in tone nor manner was there the faintest trace of the irritation he was feeling.

She smiled faintly.

"A voice!" she said. "I heard it all put into words, Mr. Tyrrell, and I knew that they were true. It was at the garden party — not a likely place to hear the truth about oneself." The voice died away, and she looked as though she were listening again to the words she had heard; and then, for the first time, her white face quivered and trembled, and she covered it suddenly with her hands. "I did not know," she cried, low and brokenly. "I never thought! I never thought! Oh! if it should be too late!"

She stopped, and there was a silence. Tyrrell was thinking that, after all, the fate that had nullified all his plans might be his best friend. His eyes were very bright and keen, as they rested on the dark, bowed head before him; he calculating the chances for and against him swiftly and resolutely, and he determined to make his move.

He rose quietly and stood beside her, resting one hand on the back of her chair.

"It is not too late, Selma," he said. "Your life is all before you still, and you will not throw it away. What you have heard to give you this pain I do not know, but I do know that it cannot have been the truth." He waited, half expecting that she would protest; but she did not speak or look up at him, though her hands had fallen from her face. They were tightly clasped in her lap, and she seemed to shrink a little as he stood over her, and rather to suffer than to listen to his words.

"The truth is this," he went on, very gently. "You are young, Selma, and the admiration and popularity you are so hard upon came to you very suddenly. You have been over-excited and over-tired, and perhaps you have, as you say, thought less than you will do for the future about your work. Selma, you want some one to help you and take care of you."

Suddenly and abruptly, as though some

intolerable and incredible possibility were taking
definite shape, for the first time Selma rose from
her chair.   It was not surprise in her face, rather
the shock of unendurable conviction, of realisation,
which seemed more than she could bear.

A strangled gasp broke from her, and she
stretched out one hand, that trembled all at once
like a leaf, as though to keep off the something
that had broken on her in that instant.

Tyrrell took the hand firmly into both his
own, and at his touch, as suddenly as her strange
emotion had shaken her, it seemed to leave her
—to leave her turned to stone, she stood so
white and motionless.

" Selma," he said, softly, " don't let me startle
you.   What I am going to say has been part
of my life for so long that I cannot bear to
think of its coming upon you as a shock.
You have thought of me — when you have
thought of me at all—always as your friend
alone, I know.   Selma, I love you ! "   A
strong shudder ran through her frame, but she

did not speak. Her face was like a marble mask, and, as he looked at it, Tyrrell changed colour slightly. "I won't ask you," he said, "to give me love, as yet. Give me the right to help you, Selma. Be my wife!"

"I am sorry, Mr. Tyrrell. It is quite impossible."

She spoke the few words coldly and quietly, drawing away her hand from his astonished hold, and moving to the other side of the room, leaving Tyrrell absolutely rooted to the ground in his amazement—not so much at the refusal itself as at the manner of it. A moment passed, at least, before he could recover himself sufficiently to find any words, and then he said, speaking almost as quietly as she had done:

"Impossible, Selma! That is a hard word. At least you will tell me why it is impossible."

There was a moment's pause, and then Selma responded in the same unnatural, unmoved tone:

"I do not love you, Mr. Tyrrell."

"That is no reason," he returned, quickly, crossing the room towards her. "I do not ask you to love me yet. Marry me, and that will come with time."

"I cannot."

"But give me a reason. Tell me why you cannot. Selma, is that so much for your old friend to ask? Tell me why."

"I have told you."

She drew back from his outstretched hands as she spoke; and, as he realised the determination in her tone, as he realised that he was failing, that she was slipping from his grasp, a passion such as he had never felt for her before seized him and carried him beyond his own self-control.

"You have not!" he cried. "It is no reason. If I am willing to wait for your love, why should you not give me all I ask? I love you, Selma, I love you, and I would win your love in time."

"Never!"

The word came from her in a low, vibrating tone which yet seemed to fill the room, and Tyrrell took a rapid step towards her.

"It is given, then, to another man!" he said, and he caught her hand in his.

Even as he touched her, Selma wrenched herself from his hold, and turned upon him at last, her eyes blazing, her whole face alight and aglow with passion.

"Given!" she cried. "Oh, have we known nothing, absolutely nothing, of each other all these years? Is there no sympathy, no comprehension in the world? Given! Oh, Roger, Roger! It was his when I sent him out of my life, though I was a child, and I didn't know what it meant. Ah, I have known since! I loved him then, I love him now, and I shall love him till I die. Given! You think lightly of a woman's love, Mr. Tyrrell. You believe that she can give it, and recall it, and give it again, as though it were a plaything. You are wrong, you are wrong! Women are not all——"

She stopped abruptly, looking at him for a moment with something like horror in her eyes, and then the colour rushed over her face again, and she clasped her hands over it.

There was no answer. Speechless and motionless, Tyrrell stood before her self-convicted and helpless. He had misunderstood. His premises were false, his calculations were false, and for the moment his brain-power availed him nothing. The doubt as to whether he had really fathomed her, which had touched him earlier in their interview, had risen suddenly into irresistible conviction to strike him dumb. The contrast between the petty sentiments of wounded pride and girlish disappointment which he had attributed to her, and the strong, enduring force of the woman's love with which he was now face to face, utterly overwhelmed him. It seemed to him that many moments passed—though he made no effort to speak — before Selma slowly lifted her face, quite white now.

" You have made a mistake, Mr. Tyrrell ! "
she said, bitterly.   " You have held love cheap,
as you have held art cheap—as I have held
art cheap.   Oh ! " she cried, suddenly, clasping
her hands passionately, " have I broken my own
heart for nothing—for nothing ?   Have I lost
it all—work and art as well as love ?   Is there
nothing before me but the mockery I have
now ?   I trusted you, Mr. Tyrrell ; I trusted
you in this as I trusted you in everything, and
every way——"   She broke off again, and again
there was the same horror in her eyes.   " You
told me it was the way," she went on, and the
words were a cry of despairing reproach.   " You
told me, and I believed you !   What did I care
for society and excitement ?   What did I care
for anything when I knew that I had lost him
for ever ?   Success was nothing to me—it never
had been anything.   Shall I ever forget that
first success when I realised that nothing could
ever take his place ?   And afterwards there was
no hope for me—none—but to do what I had

thrown away my happiness that I might do. I
had sacrificed my love in the service of art.
What did it matter to me how I worked? All I
hoped for was forgetfulness!"

The words broke away into a wailing cry,
and the face of the man before her—as white
now as her own—twitched painfully.

"And now I have lost everything," she
cried. "I sacrificed my love to art, and I sacrificed art to its counterfeit. I have lost you too!
I trusted you, and I respected you, and it is all
over. I have nothing, and I am nothing, and I
have wronged and degraded the two things I
held most sacred. But my faith in them remains!
It shall remain! It shall! And I will hold to
that. It can't be that I have spoilt my life for
a delusion after all! There must be—I know
there is—a truth and a reality in art, and I will
find it and stand on it! It is lowering to love
to let its suffering spoil one's life. I will not
lower it, for it shall make me strong."

She lifted her face as she spoke, agonised

and quivering with her passionate struggle
to grasp and hold to the truth she had
asserted with such desperate insistance. As
he looked at her, all Tyrrell's better nature
rose within him and he loved her. The next
moment her eyes fell upon his face, she
dropped her hands with a gesture of despair,
as though her strength were gone.

"It's all gone at once!" she cried, brokenly.
"Everything is gone together—everything!"

And then there was a long silence.

There was no sound of any kind in the
room. Selma had sunk into a chair, her face
hidden, and Tyrrell had turned mechanically
and walked to the window. The soft summer
air floated into the room, the summer sunlight
moved along the wall, and by-and-by, from
the hall, came the voice of little Helen,
brought in again from her walk. How long
the stillness lasted Tyrrell never knew. He
only knew that he was face to face with
what he had not seen for many years—

himself as he really was. He only knew
that he was not worthy to touch the hand
of the girl who had shown him the truth,
and that he loved her.

"If she knew all of me," he said to himself. "If she knew all!"

At last, with a face so grey and drawn
as to be hardly recognisable, he turned and
looked at her. He had made no calculation,
no plans; he had no thought left for effect.
He waited a moment more, not to consider,
but to control himself, and then he crossed
the room and stood beside her.

"You have shown me the truth," he said,
in a voice so low and broken that it hardly
sounded like John Tyrrell's voice at all. "I
cannot defend myself, even if I wished it.
Selma, I cannot help you — help me. Don't
send me away for ever from the purity and
truth I see in you. Give me some hope
that some day in the future, when your love
grows, not less, but less intensely present

with you, you will think of me — you will
let me ask you once again to be my wife.
Selma, have pity on me!"

She was half lying, half sitting, her hands
clasped against the low back of her chair, her
face hidden on them; as he spoke, her head
had fallen lower and lower, and her whole
form had seemed to collapse and shrink as if
in an agony of distress. He finished, and she
lifted her head and turned to him suddenly;
her eyes were large and beautiful with pity
and anguish, and her tears were falling fast.

"Ah!" she cried, "Mr. Tyrrell, don't speak
to me like that! I cannot bear it. Oh, I have
looked up to you all my life, I have thought
you everything that is good, and strong, and
true! I cannot bear to see you lowered!
Oh, Mr. Tyrrell!" She stretched out her
hands as she spoke his name with a cry in
which all the love and reverence of her girl-
hood were blended with a great pity and
grief; but as he stretched out his own hands

to take hers, she shrank back suddenly and dropped her face again upon the cushions of her chair.

He came a step nearer.

"Selma," he said again, hoarsely.   "Selma, have pity on me."

"Pity!" she cried.   "Oh, have I not pity? Everything is more bitter because of this; everything is harder and more hopeless to me because this has come to me too—the loss of you, the loss of my faith in my friend.   Is not my heart almost breaking with pity and shame?   But I can never be your wife, Mr. Tyrrell!   Never, never, never!"

As she said the word shame, a ghastly change had come over Tyrrell's face.   He did not move, but he stood gazing down upon her as she lay with her face hidden from him with something rigid and strained about every line of him.   As she finished, one word came from him in a harsh, hoarse voice—the voice of a man who meant to be answered.   "Why?"

"I have had—a letter."

Her face was pressed so closely to the cushion, that the words were hardly audible, and she shrank further and further into the depth of the chair.

"From——?"

"Lady Latter!"

The two words came from her in a choked, hardly articulate whisper, and having uttered them she lay crushed tightly against the cushions, her face pressed down on them, her fingers driven into them, and clinging to them as though she would never raise herself again.

There was a moment during which John Tyrrell seemed to collapse and lose his presence and his stature as he stood, and then he turned and left the room.

CHAPTER IX.

It was a lovely summer morning, with a soft haze resting over everything, and enhancing the beauty which seemed to lie behind it.

On one of the upper reaches of the Thames stood a little inn, with an external air of having established itself in its present position more for the sake of quiet than with a view to custom, so lonely and sylvan were its surroundings, and here, through the haze, the sun was shining gloriously. It shone upon the green woods and gently rising hills between which the little thatched house nestled; it shone on the quaint casement windows and on the roses and honeysuckle climbing round them; it shone on the fresh green grass which sloped down to the river; and it shone on the sparkling water, moving softly along, blue and beautiful with the reflection of the unclouded sky above.

A hundred yards or more below the garden, fragrant with its stocks and mignonette, the river was crossed by a bridge, and on the bridge, with his arms resting on the low stone parapet, gazing straight before him, far beyond the point where the river took a sudden turn, stood John Tyrrell.

He was quite alone in the morning stillness, and he had been standing there alone since six o'clock—nearly an hour ago. He was as unconscious of the passing of time as he was of the gradually increasing beauty about him —as he was of everything but the thoughts which had kept him now for the third night almost without sleep.

" You have made a mistake ! "

Had the words been really spoken to him, he was wondering heavily now as he stared at the bright blue waters, or had they come

from his own inner consciousness? They were
part of his life now; he seemed to have lived
with them for longer than he could remember.
Selma had said them to him, had she not?
"'You have made a mistake, Mr. Tyrrell!'"
No, he had said them to himself. "You have
made a mistake, John Tyrrell; a mistake! It
is all——"

"Hullo, Tyrrell! Breakfast!"

The quiet of the morning was broken by a
cheery man's voice. Two men had come to
the porch of the little inn, and the elder of the
two had shouted his announcement to Tyrrell
in jolly, stentorian tones. Tyrrell took his arms
mechanically from the parapet.

"Coming," he said, and, as he moved, the
second man, a tall, sunburnt young fellow, said
in a low voice to his companion:

"He looks most awfully ill, Roberts. How
rummy his voice is! What made him come?
I shouldn't have thought this kind of thing
was much in his line."

"I met him yesterday in Bond Street," returned the other. "He looked so ghastly that I thought it would do him good, and I told him he could moon about and do just as he liked. I believe he said 'Yes' because he didn't care enough to say 'No.' He's a good sort at the bottom. He pulled me out of a bad hole once upon a time, young fellow, before he was such a swell. Well, old man," he went on, raising his voice, as Tyrrell came up to them, "neat thing in mornings, isn't it?"

"Lovely," responded Tyrrell. He was strangely haggard, and his eyes had a curious, set expression as if, as Dick Clayton said wonderingly to himself, he were listening to something. But his manner, if it was a shade mechanical, was easy and courteous.

"I won't say breakfast is waiting!" said Miles Roberts, with a cheery laugh. "The other fellows are at it! But our breakfast is waiting. I brought this fellow out with me to look you up that we might have a look in eventually."

To this reference to his appetite, a standing joke with the party, Dick Clayton replied with a playful punch, and more or less fell into the room where breakfast was going on.

There were some half-dozen men there—it being a joint-stock affair in which Tyrrell was the guest of Miles Roberts, who was a friend of Tyrrell's early manhood, and of whom he never lost sight, though they met seldom enough. They were all more or less well known in literary or artistic lines, and they belonged to a set with which Tyrrell had never quite lost touch, though it was remote enough from the fashionable cliques of which he was one of the centres. The breakfast was jovial and noisy, if Tyrrell's words were few; but it was natural, the other men thought, that he should not be familiar with the jokes and allusions current in a party who had spent six weeks off and on in "chaffing" one another. Such a "swell" as Tyrrell was felt by some of them to be rather an incongruous element in the party, and Miles Roberts had been a good deal reviled for the eccentric impulse of old friendliness which had moved him to introduce the said "swell." "He looked so awfully played out, poor beggar," Roberts had explained apologetically, and though his words had been received with derision, the other men, having expressed themselves freely beforehand, were cordiality itself to Tyrrell when he appeared in person, and it was with a genial desire to dispel his ignorance, that Dick Clayton called out to him when breakfast was nearly over :

"Don't be deluded by that fellow, Mr. Tyrrell. The truth is——" And there Tyrrell's attention wandered from the hilarious young voice—wandered completely and uncontrollably from the easy, noisy party.

"'I can never be your wife, Mr. Tyrrell! Never! never! never!'"

He had lost her utterly, just at the moment

when he understood her worth! He had lost her for ever! Nothing—no years, no effort, no repentance—could help him! There was that between them which could never be bridged, which she could never forget. And she might have married him, he told himself calmly— she had pitied him, and she had once respected him. She might have married him if it had not been for—that.

The laughter and talk about him seemed to have withdrawn to a great distance, and to make a mocking background to his busy thoughts. He was not conscious that he answered Dick Clayton, mechanically and at random, though not perceptibly so; he was not conscious that he rose with the other men from the table, and stood about with them on the grass in front of the house; he was not conscious of wandering away from them presently along the bank of the river.

The other men smoked their pipes and cigars and chatted among themselves, and they

hardly noticed his departure until Miles Roberts
said, looking round carelessly :

"Any one see where Tyrrell went off to?
He'll turn up for lunch, I suppose."

He was out of sight by that time, walking
slowly with heavy, regular movements like a
man who is hardly conscious of bodily motion
in the active working of his mind. Everything was quite clear to him, there was nothing
left for him to think out ; but never for a
single instant were the truths which had become so distinct otherwise than present to
him.

Over and over again with a heavy, monotonous recapitulation, he went through the
story of his life as he read it now in the
light with which Selma's passionate words had
flooded it. He saw himself as he had been at
five-and-twenty, with all his life before him,
in the first glow of success ; full of artistic
enthusiasm, ambitious ; with good principles,
high faiths and impulses. He saw himself a

little later with easy success following easy success, popular and admired, with a slight dulness over his artistic ideal, a slight slackening of his artistic effort. He saw himself a society lion, appraising the adulation he received at its true worth, despising his admirers, despising the whole system at the bottom of his heart, but valuing the power and prosperity it brought him. He saw his artistic faiths and aims dead within him, slain by the bitter cynicism of the artist who had sold himself to society; slain so completely that only now and then did he remember that he had ever believed in that of which he now saw only the burlesque and travesty—art not as a means to a material end, but with a living soul. He had spent his life for a delusion and a lie, he had wasted his power, wasted his strength and his manhood, and all that he had valued was—nothing!

" 'You have made a mistake, Mr. Tyrrell!' "

He stood still as unconsciously as he had

moved forward, and he saw, not the fair summer landscape before him, but a beautiful white
face with dark flashing eyes, which seemed to
look into his across an impassable barrier of
shame and wrong. More than once during the
two days that had passed since his interview
with Selma he had had the same sensation—as
though that visionary face were burning into his
brain and shutting out everything tangible and
real. It passed again, and he resumed his
mechanical walk and his monotonous thoughts.

He had lost her! He had read her by
his own false, clouded lights; he had dragged
her down to his own level, had schemed, and
planned, and waited, and in the very intricacy of
his calculations had defeated his own ends. If
he had been capable of understanding a nature
so much higher than his own, if he had been
capable of loving her four years ago as he loved
her now, it might have been! She might have
guided him by the light that was in her to some
redemption of his past.

"'Never! never! never!'"

He ground his teeth fiercely together, and his breath came short and quick. Never! He had put himself beyond the pale. She might forgive him, she might pity him, she might come in time to think of him tenderly as of her oldest friend whom she had once respected, but she would never let him take her in his arms, she would hardly let him touch her hand ever again. He knew it! The light had been long in coming to Tyrrell, but it was relentless in its brightness now that it had come. He realised that there is one thing that such a woman as Selma never forgets, never condones, and he knew that there was no hope for him. A dark, insolent woman's face rose before his eyes, and he ground his teeth afresh with impotent self-contempt and fury, and then the beautiful white face was there again with the horror-filled, shamed eyes, and he reeled for a moment heavily against a tree.

It passed again suddenly as a boat came swiftly down the river, the quick rhythmic dip

of the oars, the laughter and talk of the men
in it—Miles Roberts, and two more—breaking
the stillness.

"Come aboard, Tyrrell," called out Roberts,
as the rowers rested on their oars and backed
gently, as the tide would have drifted them on;
"there's a splendid stream on, and it's lunch-time.
Come on!"

"Thanks," answered Tyrrell, "Bring her
in a little more." He swung himself off the
bank into the boat, saying, as the oars flashed
in the sunlight again, "Have you been
far?"

He took his share in the talk that followed,
entering easily and naturally into all that passed,
and though Miles Roberts thought once or twice
that his eyes looked "odd," their expression
told him nothing. He did not dream—not one
of the men who laughed and talked to Tyrrell
during lunch imagined—that his interest and
amusement were the surface of depths of incessantly moving, hopeless thought, that he

moved and talked through it, as it were, with the mechanical action of habit.

"Who is going to do what this afternoon?" enquired Dick Clayton, as they rose from lunch. "I am going to lie on my back in a punt under the bank."

"I will come and help you, Dick!" said Miles Roberts. "Lazy young beggar! Tyrrell, will a punt be about your form? It's very hot!"

Tyrrell was standing looking absently at the ground. He had dropped out of the conversation during the last few moments, and his consciousness had drifted away. He started as Miles Roberts turned to him, and said, lightly:

"It is hot, but I think I'll go for a row."

Twenty minutes more passed during which he heard and answered words and jests with the same curious double consciousness, and then he found himself seated alone in a boat, being cast off by Dick Clayton, under the superintendence of Miles Roberts.

" You'll find us under the trees higher up
when you come down," called Miles Roberts
after him. " We moor opposite the weir, that
Dick may be lulled to sleep."

They stood a moment watching as he got the
boat out of the stream—he was going up the
river—with a few strong, easy strokes, and
then Dick Clayton exclaimed with a whistle,
" Great Scott! he'll be hot. How he's going
it ! "

Tyrrell had bent to his sculls suddenly,
and he was rowing with all the strength and
science of which he was a master. The boat
shot on and on, and he rowed always harder
and harder, as though some mental relief were
to be hoped from the intense physical exertion,
until every nerve and muscle were strained to the
utmost, and he was rowing desperately. Mile
after mile flew by—one, two, three—and then as
suddenly as he had begun, he stopped.

It was useless ! Not for a single instant
had his mental consciousness been lessened ; and

now that beautiful white face was before him again, and he held the sculls suspended over the water, and sat gazing into the dark eyes. The boat drifted slowly into the stream, was turned gradually, and began to float gently down the river, and still the eyes held him, and he sat there motionless. Then the face faded, he unshipped the sculls mechanically, and let the boat drift with the current as he sat with idle hands, gazing before him with unseeing, hopeless eyes. What was the use of fighting or struggling? There was not a chance for him anywhere. His life lay all behind him, wasted. The future— there was no future in his thoughts, nothing but vain regret! The boat slipped softly down the stream, the green banks glided by, the river murmured gently, and he was quite unconscious of any of these things — of anything but the dreariness of utter hopelessness. Presently a boat passed him, and he met another coming up; but he never heard the energetic adjurations showered on him. Two hours passed, and his position was unchanged. His very thoughts were stationary. There was no hope for him —he had no other consciousness than that.

" You have made a mistake, a mistake, mistake ! "

The river had been singing the words in a soft, monotonous chant. What made it suddenly rise and shout them with a confused rush of sound ? The boat had been moving smoothly to the monotonous chant. Why did she suddenly stop and shiver ? Why ?

He lifted his head suddenly. Straight ahead of him, leaping and dancing in tumultuous confusion in the afternoon sunshine, were the waters of the weir above the bridge on which he had stood that morning. The boat was already caught in the current, and he was drifting swiftly and more swiftly with every instant to his death. With a desperate impulse —the impulse to cling to life which is in every man—he seized the sculls and tried to stem the stream. It was useless, and he saw it instantly.

The scull snapped like a twig in his hand, and then he smiled.

"'You have made a mistake, Mr. Tyrrell. You have made a mistake.'"

The words were in his ears louder than the roar of the weir waters, getting nearer and nearer with a terrible rush. He heard a wild shout from under the opposite bank, and with the swift perception of such a moment he knew that it was Miles Roberts.

"Hold to the post, man! For Heaven's sake, hold to the post!"

The voices seemed to come from a far-off world, and he smiled again as he heard them. The danger-post flashed past him, the roar of the waters rose suddenly around him, and he saw nothing but a beautiful white face, heard nothing but a woman's voice:

"A mistake, a mistake!"

But the waters of death had closed over John Tyrrell, and all his mistakes were ended!

CHAPTER X.

THROUGHOUT the remainder of that summer and throughout the early part of the autumn that followed it Selma was very ill, not dangerously ill after the first, but seeming to regain little strength and to care to regain it less. The news of Tyrrell's death told to her gently by Helen, who was very anxious about her even then, seemed to break her down utterly, and she grieved for him with a grief that could find few words, and expressed itself only in the slow, heavily-dropping tears which stole down her thin white cheeks so constantly as she lay still hour after hour with weary, hopeless eyes — tears which fell for her dead trust in her friend and for the pitiful story of his life as she saw it now.

R 2

Five years had passed since then, and it was a bright afternoon early in November. Helen's drawing-room looked very dainty and pretty— not the less dainty for the fact that little Helen, growing quite a "large girl" now, as she said of herself, and two small brothers, were quite as happy there as in their nursery. Helen was sitting near the fire, talking to a lady, and nearer the window, talking to Mrs. Cornish and Humphrey, with little Helen sitting on her knee, was Selma.

She had been a beautiful girl, and she was now a most beautiful woman. Her features, always grave and quiet now, except when she was acting, were a little worn and thin, as though with past suffering or deep thought— perhaps with both.

The large, dark eyes looked larger and lovelier than ever from the slight hollowing of the setting and the faint shadows about them, and their expression was quiet and steady. There were lines about the mouth, and its girlish curves were gone for ever; but the lovely lips had acquired a dignity and sweetness which they had never worn in her youth, and as they smiled down at the child on her knee, it was no wonder that a little hand stole softly up to stroke her cheek. No child ever turned away from Selma now.

"Nothing could please me more than to hear that," she was saying, quietly, and to her voice as to her face time had brought only maturity of beauty.

"I'm not given to crying, my dear," responded Mrs. Cornish, energetically. "I'm too old to cry about nothing; but I couldn't get over it at all. My dear, you are wonderful—it's late in the day to tell you that, I know; everybody knows all about you. But I never realised it myself before."

Mrs. Cornish rose as she spoke, and the other lady who had come with her to call on Helen followed her example.

"There is nothing left for any one to say

about Miss Malet," she said, turning to Selma with a smile. "We owe her a great deal. May I thank you, at least, for your performance the other night?"

"Thank you," said Selma, courteously, with the same grave smile.

Mrs. Cornish took her into her arms, with a curious touch of respect mingled with her cordiality; and then the two ladies took leave, and departed with Helen to visit the nursery.

"You have made a conquest, Selma," said Humphrey, smiling, as the door closed upon them.

"Auntie?" said Selma, crossing to the fireplace as she spoke. "I am very pleased. Humphrey, don't you think that there is a great deal in criticism like that? I feel as though one's work must ring true to touch any one like auntie. She never reasons as to how a thing is done."

She was looking thoughtfully into the fire

as she spoke, and Humphrey watched her for
a moment before he answered her. He had
watched her a great deal during the past five
years, and all he knew now was that there
were depths in her of which he had known
nothing when he thought that her artist life
was over, and that she might marry John
Tyrrell for his money and position; depths
that he should never quite fathom; strength,
and nobility, and constancy that he could only
guess at. She was such an artist now as he
had known long ago that she might be. She
had devoted herself to her work with a curious,
steady, unexpressed reverence for it which
differed strangely from her old enthusiasm;
her genius had developed with every year;
and every year there strengthened about her
a certain atmosphere, as of a woman whose
every thought and aspiration centres round an
ideal which has, she knows, no realisation on
earth; who looks through, and beyond, the art
to which her life is given, to the perfect beauty

and completeness of which all human art is as
the faintest shadowing forth.

Her quiet life was very full, as the life
of such an artist cannot fail to be—she stood
at the head of her profession with an artistic
position which was unassailable—but Humphrey
wondered often, as he looked at her face in
repose, whether she was happy. He knew
that a certain amount of unsatisfied longing
was inevitable to the artist nature in her.
But was she as happy as she might have
been ? Was she happy as a woman ? He
had known the truth about her heart that
day, long ago, in the studio, when Mervyn
and Roger were there together; he had known
then that she loved Roger still; but he was
conscious of having been entirely mistaken in
his after judgement of her. Now he was
conscious of a certain vague pity and sympathy
as he looked at her or talked to her. Was
she content ? he wondered often. He was
wondering now rather sadly as he answered :

"I quite agree with you. Intellectual criticism is fascinating, but it is not an infallible test." He paused a moment, and then said gently, almost in spite of himself:

"Your work stands both tests, Selma— intellectual and emotional. You should be satisfied."

She lifted her eyes to him with a slight smile.

"Satisfied with my work, Humphrey?"

"Hardly that," he responded, answering her smile. "I don't wish you stagnation! Satisfied with life!"

She did not answer him at once. He thought she sighed, but the sound was very low. She had not raised her head, and was standing in the same quiet, graceful attitude, looking steadily into the fire, when there was a sudden sound of voices in the hall. Humphrey, turning quickly, did not see that Selma turned a little paler; and the next moment he had crossed the room, opened the door, and was shaking his brother Roger by both hands.

"Old boy!" he exclaimed. "When did you get back?"

"Only last night," exclaimed Helen, who was following—as Roger returned the clasp of his brother's hands with a hearty, "How are you, old fellow?"—"Isn't it nice of him to come to us to-day? And how is Mervyn? Tell us all about her," she added, delightedly, while Roger shook hands with Selma, who had come quietly forward to meet him.

Roger and Mervyn had been abroad for more than a year. Mervyn had never seemed to get over the loss of her baby, and year after year had left her more fragile and delicate, until at last—eighteen months before—the death of her father had given her a shock which led to a long illness. Her father had left her money, and when she was advised to live abroad for a year at least, Roger was able to arrange his business affairs and take her away. For many months there had been little hope of his ever bringing her back again, and his

few short letters home had been almost heart-
broken. Then there had come a change; she
had begun to gain a little strength. And now
she had come home again, as Roger assured
Helen with exuberant happiness, "The strongest
little woman in London."

"She would have come with me this afternoon," he said, "but there's some bother with
the servants. Come back with me, Helen, and
see her. She'll be so awfully pleased. I want
to show her off to you. You won't know
her."

Roger himself was altered almost as much
as Mervyn could be. He was much bronzed,
and his face was firmer and stronger for the
five years of anxiety about his little wife.
There were lines in it and a touch of grey in
the hair about his temples which aged him
and at the same time improved him greatly,
with the touch of dignity and maturer, more
thoughtful, manhood they brought him. His
blue eyes were radiant with an almost trium-

phant happiness now, however, as he turned
them upon Helen, and she answered :

"I'll come with pleasure, Roger. I'm longing to see her. Oh, I'm so glad !"

"When did you cross ?" asked Humphrey.

"By the midday boat, yesterday," answered
Roger. "Mervyn hates night journeys."

"You had a lovely day," commented Selma,
quietly. And then a servant came and spoke to
Humphrey.

"A lady in the studio, sir, to see you about
a picture."

"Very well," he responded. "What a
nuisance, Roger ! She may keep me half an
hour. You're not off in a hurry ?"

"I am, worse luck !" returned Roger, ruefully. "We must say good-bye, old man."

They stood a moment arranging a future
meeting that should not be interrupted by commissions, and then, after another tremendous
handshake, Humphrey departed, and Roger
said to Helen :

" Is it a good thing ? "

" It's splendid ! " said Helen, proudly. " He doesn't often take commissions; he says they are a tie; but he couldn't refuse this."

She told him all about it; and they talked for a little while of Humphrey and his success, coming back again to Mervyn and their travels, until Roger said, finally :

"If you really will come back with me, Helen, I think we ought to be off. She will be expecting me."

Helen rose at once. " I'll go and get ready," she said. " Selma, dear, tell me the time, if you can see the clock," and as Selma answered her she left the room.

There was a moment's silence as she shut the door—a silence which was broken by Selma.

"Did you come straight through ? It is a long journey," she said.

" We spent twenty-four hours in Paris," he answered. " Mervyn is very fond of it, and she shopped furiously all day."

He was looking at the quiet, graceful figure opposite him as he spoke, thinking how beautiful she was, and how greatly she had altered. It was a long time since he had felt as though the Selma of the day and the Selma of old were really one and the same, and now the time that had elapsed since he had seen her seemed to make him realise the difference more distinctly than he had ever done before. He could not feel as though this grave, sweet woman was the girl he had loved and lost. That girl had been the ideal of his youth, this woman was something far away from him, to be respected and admired from a distance. The two had two points in common in his mind, and only two; they were both beautiful and incomprehensible, and they were both far above him. They had another point in common, of which he was not conscious. They existed side by side in the dim background of his thoughts, while all the foreground was filled with the wife he loved.

"She was always enthusiastic over shop-

ping," said Selma, smiling at his description of
Mervyn's proceedings in Paris. "It is delightful to hear that she is strong enough for such a
hard day's work."

"It is delightful," rejoined Roger, fervently,
his whole face glowing with satisfaction.

The November afternoon was drawing in,
and the room was growing dark. The flickering
fire lighted Roger's features as he stood near it,
and Selma's eyes, as she sat in shadow, were
fixed upon him steadily.

"You are quite satisfied about her? She is
quite strong again?" she said. Her voice was
very low and sweet, and there was something in
its tone which seemed to stir the depths of
Roger's thankfulness and joy. He looked down
into the beautiful woman's face lifted to his,
seeing nothing but the sympathy he read in
it, remembering nothing but his own great
happiness.

"She is quite strong again," he said, softly.
"I can't tell you what it is to me to know it."

Selma rose, still with her eyes on his, and held out her hand gently to him.

" You are very happy ? " she said.

" I am very, very happy," he answered.

" I am glad ! " The three words came from her very softly, and an instant later Helen's voice called him from the hall ; he wrung the slender hand he held, and was gone.

" Take care of yourself, Selma ! " called Helen's voice, cheerily, as the street-door opened. Then it closed again.

Selma walked slowly across the room to the window. She could not see from it the street along which Helen and Roger were walking. She stood there, quietly looking out into the fast darkening evening—alone.

THE END.

CHARLES DICKENS AND EVANS CRYSTAL PALACE PRESS.